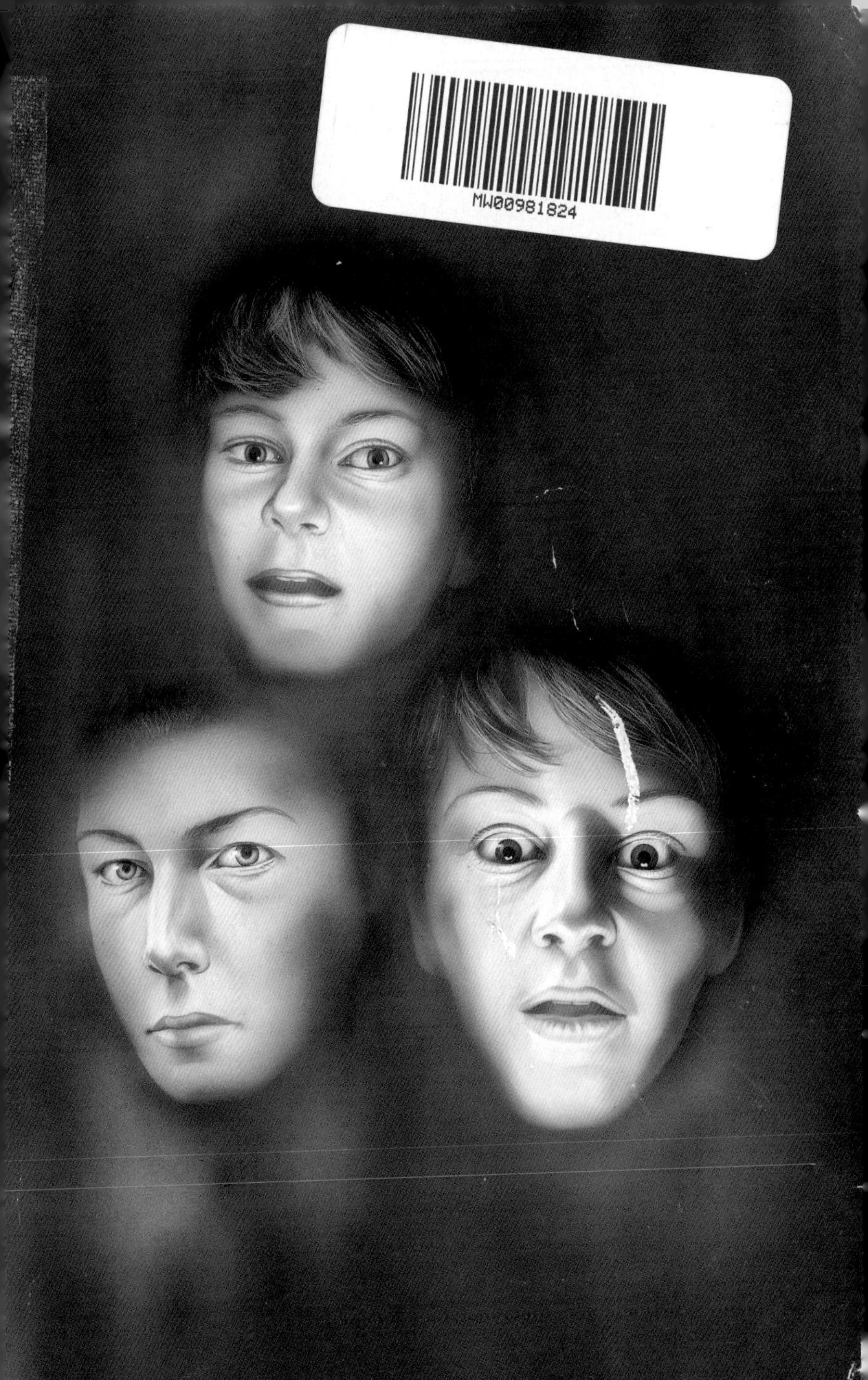
MW00981824

I'm not going in there, thought Stan, but Floella stepped inside. Stan followed, unable to make his legs obey his mind.

They were standing in an enclosed space at the foot of a steep, stone staircase. A staircase that spiralled up into the darkness above. Floella began to climb. So did Stan. Slowly...

...Five more steps to the top.

Four.

Stan's feet felt like great lumps of concrete. It took every ounce of strength to move them.

Three.

The sound of that laugh – that horrible, gloating, evil laugh – was echoing round his head.

Two.

It's not too late to turn back, a voice said in his head. *Not quite*. But deep in his heart, Stan knew that it was.

Other titles in this series coming soon...

Letters from the Grave
Destination Fear
The Mindmaster
The Clock of Doom
The Haunted Hotel
The House of Secrets
Murder at the Haunted Hotel

FACES AT THE WINDOW

Emma Fischel

First published in 1996 by Usborne Publishing Ltd, Usborne House, 83-85 Saffron Hill, London EC1N 8RT, England.

ISBN 0 7460 2472 X (paperback)

ISBN 0 7460 2473 8 (hardback)

Typeset in Palatino

Printed in Great Britain

Series Editor: Gaby Waters

Designer: Lucy Parris

Cover illustration: Barry Jones

CONTENTS

1

Explosions

"Get out!" hissed Floella. "I think it's going to explode!"

Stan edged further into the room. He wasn't missing out on this for anything.

Today had been hard going, what with the move and having to be good and helpful and not in the way all the time. One of Floella's experiments could be just what was needed to liven things up.

Floella was crouched in the centre of the room, wedging a cork into the neck of huge plastic bottle. Something brown and foamy was starting to fizz inside.

"Get back," she spat, waving him away.

Stan stayed where he was and fixed both eyes

on the bottle. He was ready to give the foaming, fizzing stuff – whatever it was – his full attention.

Something was wrong. Floella had a great big frown on her face. It looked as if things weren't going according to plan.

SPOOOOSH... The cork shot out and so did an enormous jet of brown foam. Floella jumped back, but not fast enough. It got her everywhere – in the face, in the hair and all down her front.

Then came the smell. Out of nowhere, the most disgusting, pungent horrible stench. And it was heading straight for the back of Stan's throat. He pulled his sweat shirt up over his nose and choked into it.

The brown foamy stuff was still spurting out of the bottle, fizzing its way across the salmony pink carpet and leaving splashy brown trails across the rose-patterned wallpaper.

Stan gaped. You had to hand it to Floella. It hadn't taken her long. Two hours in her new bedroom and it was already a disaster area.

Much like Floella herself. Yes, from head to foot Floella Lampkin, scientist and inventor, was a ghastly sight. Not that she noticed.

"Hmm. That wasn't meant to happen quite like that," she said, frowning down at the bottle. "I'll try again tomorrow. Is it teatime yet?"

And that, thought Stan, was Floella all over.

Ordinary things didn't matter to her the way

they did to other people. Things like whether it was fish or sausages for lunch, or how many weeks till Christmas, or who put the stick insect in Belinda Gregory's pencil case.

She could tell you the average speed of an avalanche. She knew at least a hundred interesting facts about dinosaur teeth. She could probably even build a roller-skating robot.

But ask her what day of the week it was, or what number bus went to the ice rink, and she wouldn't have a clue. She wouldn't even care.

No. Floella Amelia Lampkin had no time for ordinary things. A fact which Stan, having been her brother for his whole life and most of hers, knew all too well.

He also knew whose voice that was bellowing up at them from the hallway, and whose feet were starting to thud up the stairs. That voice and those feet belonged to none other than Alan Morris Lampkin. Dad.

Stan braced himself. You didn't have to be a rocket scientist to know that another major explosion was just around the corner.

Dad stood, open-mouthed in the doorway. He gazed slowly round the room. There was a lot of silence.

Then he looked at Floella, covered in brown streaks, standing in the middle of the room. His eyes narrowed.

Stan held his breath. Dad looked about as chummy as a man-eating tiger.

"Settled in, I see," he said, grinding his teeth.

Floella stood silently. She had nothing to say. But Dad had. He had plenty. He sucked in a great lungful of air and let rip for a good ten minutes.

Floella politely stood and listened, just as she had last week after her working model of a blizzard exploded in the freezer. But it wouldn't make any difference and they all knew it. The moment she got another brainwave that needed testing out, she'd just go ahead. You might as well try and stop a juggernaut squashing a cupcake.

In the end Dad ran out of steam. Then Floella spoke. "It'll wash off," she said calmly. "You'll see."

And she was right.

2

THE MOVE

The latest Floella fiasco had not been a good end to the day of the move, a day that had started far too early for Stan's liking, and with horrible suddenness...

... "Rise and shine!" Dad had bellowed, bursting into Stan's bedroom and flinging the curtains open.

Stan opened one eye. "It's half-term," he mumbled.

"It is also moving day!" said Dad, whisking the duvet off Stan's bed. "There's work to be done and the move starts NOW!"

The rest of the morning had passed in a frenzy. Dad was everywhere, barking out orders, handing out chores, bustling from room to room with a list of things to be done.

Stan and Floella stumbled about following order after order. They emptied cupboards, cleared shelves, packed crates. They cleaned and dusted, vacuumed and polished until they ached from head to foot. Not one single speck of dust escaped Dad's eagle eye.

By midday, number one Molehill Road was gleaming and unrecognizable. Every last thing was packed up ready for the removers. There was nothing left to do now, except say goodbye.

Stan wandered from room to room. It didn't take long. Number one Molehill Road verged on the tiny side of small. Compact, Dad had called it. Call it what you like, to Stan it was home.

All right, so the mould in the bathroom was multiplying by the minute. And the kitchen wall bulged into the sitting room. But it was *his* house. The only place he had ever lived and full of memories. Lots of them were good, some of them were bad, but all of them were hard to leave.

He stood in the kitchen. There were little marks in felt tip pen up the wall – green for him and blue for Floella, marking the date and their height and both gradually creeping higher and higher.

His eyes went all blurry. He gave a miserable sniff.

"Remembering?" Dad was behind him.

"Was I really that small?" said Stan, sniffing again.

"Smaller than that even," said his father with a croak. He sounded as if he'd swallowed a cheesegrater.

Then he tried to crack a joke. "That's one thing we'll have to leave behind. Unless we take the wall with us." He dabbed at his eyes with the corner of his sleeve, then blew his nose on his duster.

"I am pleased to be going," Stan struggled to explain. "It's just..."

"I know," said Dad. He put his arm round Stan. "I know."

Stan nodded. It was true. He was happy to be going, in lots of ways. After all, they were moving to a bigger house, a bigger garden, a new start.

And he was pleased for his father too. The house had never really been the same since Mum died... well, Stan didn't think so anyway.

"Let's get going, then," Dad said, with a squeeze of Stan's shoulder.

They took one last silent look, then walked out of the front door and closed it behind them.

Floella was already in the front seat of the car. Her nose was firmly buried in her *Inventions* notebook. She was scribbling furiously. She didn't say a word.

Stan was soon wedged in the back between the guinea pig's hutch and a pile of plastic boxes, with hard corners that dug into his ribs.

Dad put the key in the ignition. A little huddle of neighbours started to wave at them, all grouped round the lamp post that had lit Stan's room with a warm orange glow every night since he could remember.

"Wait!" shrieked a voice, and a grubby figure hurtled out of number 23 Molehill Road and raced up the street.

"Midge," said Stan, beaming. He wound down his window.

"Something for you," gasped the grubby figure, thrusting an envelope at Stan.

Stan opened it, while Dad pretended to look through his rear view mirror at the traffic. The sticky bit on the flap was still slightly soggy.

Inside there was a card, a grown up, serious sort of card, with a great bunch of red flowers in a vase on the front. The sort Dad always kept in reserve for sending to great aunts. Inside was a message, written in careful, curly joined up writing.

With all good wishes on your moveing day
Sinserely yours. Winston J. Midgeley.
better known as Midge
Friend, neighber, and classmate
PS. I enclose a further addition to your autagraph colection

There was a bus ticket inside the card with an inky splodge on the back. "The cat's pawprint," Midge explained proudly through the window. "Took me hours to get it. I had to bribe him with a sardine."

Dad started the engine and they were off. Goodbye forever to Molehill Road.

Stan cried. So did Dad, although he tried to put it down to house dust up his nose. Floella never even looked back.

3

NUMBER 40

Twenty minutes later they turned into The Glades, a leafy road of biggish smartish modern houses that all looked pretty much alike. Number 40, the last but one in the road, was no exception.

It was a step up in the world from Molehill Road all right. For a start, it was about four times the size, with wide bay windows and a front drive big enough to park a bus on.

The gravel crunched under Stan's trainers as he stepped out of the car, hot on Floella's heels. Dad was ahead of them. "Ready?" he said, producing the front door key with a flourish. Stan nodded. So did Floella.

Click. He turned the key in the lock and they were in. Dad first, then Floella followed by Stan.

It felt a bit strange to Stan, being in the hallway. Exciting too. He'd been here before, to visit, but this time it was different. This time it was theirs.

"Let's take it from the top," said Dad, bounding towards the stairs.

They all roared around the four big empty rooms upstairs, deciding whose was whose and what went where. Then they turned their attention to the bathroom, a swanky royal blue affair with gold taps and mirror tiles and, right now, flooded with sunlight.

"You could fit the school swimming team in there," said Stan, gaping down into the bath.

"And the reserves in the shower," said Dad.

Floella wasn't listening. She had found something. A solitary glass bottle with a handwritten label, about the only thing the previous owners had left behind. It looked like antiseptic or something from the first aid kit at school.

Floella was sniffing it and wrinkling up her nose. She looked preoccupied. Stan knew that look. It was bad news. It meant she was plotting something, probably something messy, smelly or noisy; almost certainly something Dad wasn't going to like. "Carry on without me," she said, hurrying off to her new bedroom.

Dad and Stan turned their attention downstairs, to the three big rooms and one small one that made up the ground floor. Dad wasted no time. Straight off he slapped a label on the door to the small room.

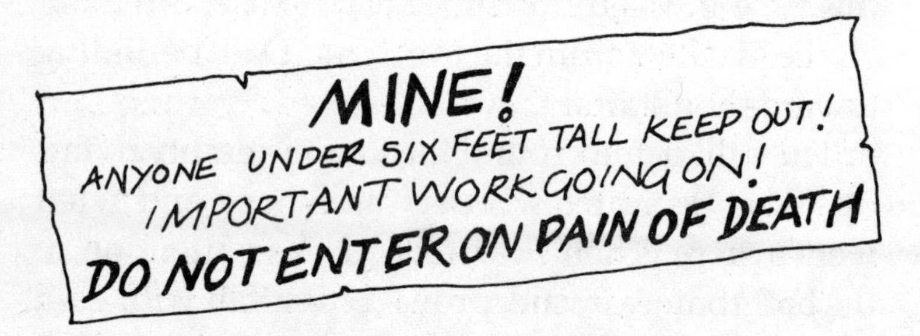

Stan could picture it already. He gave it one week – maximum – before the room was strewn with paper. Sheets and sheets of it, all covered with writing, mostly crossed out. Dad would be busy on another hot news story.

Things had been looking up lately for Dad. It was all down to an award-winning piece on graffiti in school playgrounds he had written for the *Daily Enquirer.* Within days he had TV people phoning up, wanting to turn it into a docudrama.

Within weeks he was in demand.

No more reports on record slug sightings for *Greenfingers Weekly* since then. No more shock-horror exposures of truancy among teachers during heat waves for *Chatter Magazine*. No more stories on church jumble sales and missing gerbils for the local paper, the *Riverditch News*.

These days it was quality writing for quality publications. And up until now, all done from a corner of the sitting room in Molehill Road. But no longer. At last Dad, also known as A.M. Lampkin, freelance journalist, was the proud owner of a room he could call his own.

Three hours after they first arrived, Stan and Dad called a halt and slumped in the kitchen. Dad looked at his watch. "Feeding time," he said. "Tell Floella she's got five minutes."

And that was the point at which Stan had stumbled upon Floella and her doomed exploding experiment. Things had been a bit frosty all evening after that.

Stan wiped a last blob of peanut butter off his chin and stood up. "Goodnight, then," he said with a big yawn.

He shifted from foot to foot – a tricky moment, this one. Maybe tonight could be a new start. Maybe tonight could be retirement time for the goodnight kiss.

Stan shuffled about. How could he put it, though? He didn't want to upset his father. Not today.

He loved Dad, of course. In fact, as fathers went, his was probably as good as you could hope to get. But a goodnight kiss... Stan was getting a bit, well, *old* for that sort of thing.

"Goodnight, then," said Dad. He looked at Stan but didn't move.

Stan was puzzled. Dad was just sitting there – how come? He always stood up and plonked a kiss on Stan's forehead. Every night without fail.

Dad smiled. "Off you go, then," he said, still not budging.

He knows, thought Stan. He can read my mind.

"Right. Err. Goodnight then," Stan said, heading for the stairs. He could hardly believe it.

On an impulse, he turned around at the bottom of the stairs. "It'll be good here, Dad, this house," he said. "I know it will."

Dad smiled. "I hope so, Stan. I hope so."

Stan started up the stairs. Then he heard his father's voice behind him. "Stan. Haven't you forgotten something?"

Stan spun around. He knew it. It was too good to be true. Dad had remembered after all.

"Watch out for ghosts," said Dad, smiling. Then he blew Stan a kiss.

And winked.

The stairs creaked under Stan's feet. There was nothing to absorb the noise, just bare walls and bare floors.

Houses need people, thought Stan. People and their things. Without people in them, their things, their laughter, a house is nothing. Worse than nothing – cold and lonely, like a person without a heart or feelings.

The door to his room was open. Inside the room was dark. Stan flicked on the light as he went in, then shut the door behind him.

It was a big square room with a big square window looking out over the back garden. The rain was starting to patter against the window pane. Stan turned to look out.

His eyes travelled down the garden, over the tangle of trees behind, up to the big, old house beyond. He'd seen the house before, just a glimpse really. That was when they'd first visited The Glades, but it had been summer then and the trees had hidden all but the roof-top and chimneys. No one lived there Dad had said. It was empty, had been for years.

Now most of the leaves had fallen off the trees, it was clearly visible – or would be by daylight. Through the rain, under the glimmer of the blue-white moon, Stan could just make out the dark shape of a vast building, more like an ancient castle than a house. Not a flicker of light. No sign of life.

He turned away. Something about the way it stood there, all alone, all black and crooked against the skyline, made him feel uneasy. Almost threatened.

Stan got ready for bed. Tomorrow he would ask Dad to put up some curtains.

He lay down. His old bed and stripy duvet felt

reassuringly familiar in this new room with its unfamiliar shadows. It was much quieter here than at Molehill Road. No cars taking a short cut through to the main road going north. No minicabs honking their horns outside the Bell and Trumpet. Just the occasional purr of a well-serviced engine gliding slowly down a distant road.

They could have been the only house for miles around for all that Stan could hear from outside.

Stan's thoughts were beginning to wander. He was tired, so tired. A faint rumble of thunder drifted into the room, but his eyes were already closing. Seconds later, he drifted off to sleep.

If Stan had stayed awake long enough, he would have heard the thunderstorm creep nearer and nearer. He would have heard the thunder grow louder. And he would have seen, in the darkest hour of the night, the lightning cut jagged white lines through the sky.

If Stan had stayed awake long enough...

But Stan had sunk into a deep and dreamless sleep, where he knew nothing of the violent storms of the night, nor of the terrors that were to follow.

4

HOME ALONE

Dad gave every appearance of having been up for hours by the time Stan made it downstairs the next morning. Bristling with energy, he was whistling and bustling his way around the kitchen.

Stan and Floella ate their breakfast in silence. Stan had an uneasy feeling about Dad. It looked suspiciously as if he had PLANS for them.

"I'm off shopping," said Dad, leaping up, car keys jangling in his hand. "I'll be back by lunchtime. Floella, while I'm out, I want you to..."

"Sorry," said Floella, slicing her toast into four equilateral triangles. "Whatever it is, I can't. I'm meeting Margery, remember?"

"Hmmm," Dad muttered without enthusiasm.

He hadn't remembered.

"You did say I could," Floella went on. But that was before yesterday's fiasco, thought Stan.

"Slime collecting. For my next experiment," she explained, putting a collection of jam jars labelled *SLIME SAMPLES* into a bag.

Yesterday's lecture obviously hadn't worked any better than the ones before. "Floella," said Dad, trying a calm and reasonable manner. "When you get back, I'd like you to..."

"Yes, yes, yes I promise," she said, pulling on her boots. "Can't stop now. I'm meeting Margery at nine."

Dad's patient tones didn't fool Stan. He wasn't happy. His face was all scrunched up and frowny. He would have been a worthy contestant in the Mr. Mean competition Belinda Gregory had organized in the lunch hour last Tuesday.

"So I'll see you this evening," continued Floella, squashing equilateral triangle number four into her mouth.

"In time for tea. Six o'clock," said Dad, firmly. "At the latest!"

"Byeeee," called Floella, with a little wave. Then she was gone.

Stan sighed. Typical Floella, waltzing off like that. And no prizes for guessing what would happen next. He gave it five seconds.

Four. Three. Two. One.

"Stan," said Dad, right on cue. "I want every crate in that room of yours unpacked by the time I get back! Understood?" With that, he zoomed off in the car before Stan could say a word.

Stan trudged off upstairs and plonked himself down on his bed. Some day this was turning out to be, stuck in his room with a load of packing cases that would probably reach to Mars and back stacked on top of each other.

Brilliant.

He shivered. It felt colder all of a sudden. Outside, the sky was growing dark and gloomy with swelling grey clouds. Then the first drops of rain started to spatter against the window.

He headed for the first crate, the one that had been dumped beside his bed. Perched on the top was the clown mask Auntie Joy had given him. That could go on the hook at the back of the door, underneath his dressing gown.

Next he pulled out a photo of himself dressed as a pink dragon in his first-ever school play and some stupid drawings he'd done when he was younger. He tossed them onto the bed. He'd find somewhere for them later. Then he dug down a little deeper.

He rummaged around amongst a mass of soft furry things. Then his hand felt something hard. He cheered up immediately. Now here was something that deserved a prime site on his wall.

This is to certify that

Stanley Arthur Lampkin

wrote a

bloodcurdlingly

spinetinglingly

gruesomely

ghastly

story called

The Wailing Ghost in the Wardrobe

that really made us

SCRE-E-EAM!

Signed in blood by

H. P. Scream

for SCREAM CITY

Stan buffed the glass with his sleeve.

This was his one and only certificate, apart from the one he got when he was six and did a soppy dance at the Riverditch Arts Festival. That didn't really count though – all the six year olds had got one, even the little podge with two left feet who picked her nose the entire way through.

No, this certificate was really something special. He had won it only a few weeks before. It had been a promotional thing for a new shop in the High Street, Scream City.

His prize was a stash of vouchers to spend in Scream City. He made the *Riverditch News* too – a full page article with a photo. Dad swore he had nothing to do with it. Stan wasn't so sure.

But in a funny way, the certificate had been the best part of all, something he could be really proud of. Stan hung it up over his bed and stood back. Perfect.

Next he took out his books, the ones bought with his prize vouchers first. It had taken him hours to choose them. He'd happily have had every book in the shop. Stories of terror and fear, of mystery and imagination, eerie tales of ghosts and ghouls, of phantoms with evil powers. He couldn't get enough of them.

Dad wasn't so keen on Stan's choice of books, said he was worried Stan would give himself nightmares. But Dad didn't seem to understand.

Things like that didn't frighten Stan, not a bit of it. They thrilled him, they sent shivers down his spine, but they didn't frighten him.

Something like not having done his homework for Blodgett, now that was scary. Being forced to eat school rice pudding, waiting for an injection, having to play a duet with Belinda Gregory in front of the whole class.

Those things were frightening. Real things. Real horrors. Not monsters and ghouls and wailing ghosts in the wardrobe.

Stan hummed quietly as he laid all his books out on the floor. He looked at his watch. Twelve o'clock on the dot. Dad would be back soon.

Outside he could hear the wind starting to moan in the trees. The rain was spattering against the window pane, harder and harder.

Stan looked out. Beyond the bare, dark branches of the trees at the end of the garden, he could see that house again. There were windows everywhere, small, dark windows, like a mass of blank staring eyes keeping watch through the trees.

Then Stan thought he saw something else. He pressed his nose to the window for a closer look. Yes. Now he could see it. A face. There was a face looking out of one of the windows – a narrow, arched window, different from the rest, set high up under the eaves.

Stan looked away. He shook his head. So, there

was a face there. Big deal. Someone probably lived there after all. Perhaps Dad had been wrong. He laughed uneasily. That had taken him by surprise, all right.

But something made him turn round and look again. Something, he couldn't say what, drew him back again.

The face was still there.

It was a boy's face, about his own age. An ordinary sort of face, nothing special. Except...

Stan blinked. His heart started to beat a little faster. Something was wrong.

It was crazy. That boy must be standing at a window at least a hundred yards away, maybe more. Yet, through the rain and the trees, he could see his face clearly. So clearly he felt he could almost reach out and touch it.

But it was more than that. The face wasn't moving. That was it, not moving an inch. Not a blink or a breath, not a flicker of expression passed over it. Nothing.

The boy's face seemed to be staring at Stan. Not seeing him, but looking straight through him. Not seeing *anything*, just looking out of the window through blank and staring eyes. Real yet unreal, like a picture.

Then it was gone. Vanished. One moment the face was staring at him, the next it had gone. Stan didn't even realize he'd blinked, but he supposed that's what he must have done. Laughing feebly, he turned away. His heart was pounding away like a hammer inside his chest.

Ridiculous. Maybe he was imagining things.

Toot, toot! Dad was back. Stan ran out of his room and dashed down the stairs, two at a time. Dad was walking through the front door clutching two pizzas. Good. Now he could forget about that face at the window.

He tried, he tried all day, but it kept coming back to him. Eating pizza, watching TV, cleaning his teeth, at all sorts of moments he would see an image of that blank staring face.

Something about the way it had looked made it impossible to get out of his head. Something – but if you had asked him, he wouldn't have been able to say quite what.

And it took him almost until bedtime to ask Dad the question he'd been wanting to ask ever since lunchtime. "You know that old house at the back, the one you said..."

"Mmmm," his father replied, nose buried in a seed catalogue.

"Is it really empty?" Stan blurted out. "I mean deserted."

"As far I know," said Dad. "The gates have been boarded up and padlocked ever since... since, oh, years back." Now he was peering at a double page of climbing roses.

"So no one lives there?" Stan asked, just one more time to be certain. "Or even goes there?"

Dad looked up again. He had his almost-patient expression on his face. "I shouldn't think so. Not with those locks on the gates..." He paused for a moment. "Why?"

"Oh," Stan was taken by surprise. "Nothing. Just wondered," he lied. For some reason, he couldn't quite bring himself to tell his father about the strange face at the window. Dad would only tell him he was imagining things, probably pin the blame on all the stuff Stan read. He could hear him now: "Too many scary stories, that's your trouble." Maybe he'd be right.

All the same, when Stan climbed the stairs to his room that night, he was sure of one thing. He didn't want to look outside again. He didn't want to see the old house.

He didn't even want to think about it.

He switched out the light and lay in the dark. He closed his eyes, but sleep was a million miles away. His mind kept returning to the arched window and the face with the blank, staring eyes.

There's nothing to see out there, he told himself. Just the garden and the trees and a big, empty house. Yes, just an empty house. Nothing more.

Sleep still wouldn't come.

He sat up. He didn't want to look out of the window... but he had to. He had to see for himself.

He looked and looked again. Nothing. All the same, Stan shuddered. Silhouetted in the light of the moon, the old house looked huge and hunched, like a crouching monster waiting to spring.

Stan buried his face in the pillow.

5

IN THE NEWS

"Fish-pond... a whole family of frogs... don't you?... in the hydrangeas, of all places..." Stray snatches of conversation were drifting into Stan's room from the garden. His father's voice and another one Stan didn't recognize.

He stretched, then yawned. He was awake – just. He got out of bed and padded over to the window. The rain had stopped and the sky was clear.

Below him, the garden sloped gently away. It was a long, thin, neat sort of garden with a patio made of coloured paving slabs and a brick barbecue at the top. In the middle was a lawn, now strewn with brown autumn leaves, neatly shaped flowerbeds down either side, a fish-pond and, down at the bottom, a potting shed. A high wooden fence kept the tangled woods beyond at bay.

Stan stared down the garden. One set of footprints had pressed dark shapes into the wet lawn – hulking great footprints that led all the way down the garden.

Stan only knew one person with feet that size. Dad. And there he stood at the bottom of the garden, talking over the hedge to what must be their neighbour at number 42.

Stan frowned. It would be just his luck if she turned out to be a *mentioner*, like Mr. Millett in Molehill Road had been.

"Just thought I'd *mention*, Mr. Lampkin, that I saw Stanley kick his football into number three's greenhouse." Or, "Just thought I'd *mention*, Mr. Lampkin, that young Stanley roller-skated into number seven's new front gate last week."

Stan had hardly been able to breathe without Mr. Millett mentioning it to his father. He could do without another one of those living next door. Stan peered down at her. Mentioner or not, she and Dad seemed to be getting on like a house on fire.

Stan turned away from the window. It was time to get dressed. Time for breakfast. He started to whistle.

You didn't look up, said a small voice in his head. *You didn't look up at the house.* Stan bent down to do up his trainers.

You're still doing it, taunted the small voice in his head. *Keeping your back to the window, not looking round.*

Stan straightened up. Of course there was some perfectly simple explanation for what he'd seen yesterday. Yes, some simple explanation for the whole thing. There had to be. It stood to reason.

So turn round, insisted the voice. *Do it.*

Stan did it. He turned round and looked. Then he looked again... and laughed with relief.

So much for being scared. It was just a house. Very big. Very old. Very empty.

As for the face, it couldn't have been a *real* face that he'd seen. Not from that distance. Of course not. It was raining remember. It was probably one of those... what was it called? He racked his brains. A phenomenon. That was it. Something to do with freak weather conditions, a trick of the light, or something like that.

No, thought Stan, marching towards the stairs, there was nothing sinister about the old house. Or about the face at that high arched window.

Nothing at all.

The sun streamed in through the big kitchen window. It flooded the room with light and bounced off the walls. The radio was playing some stirring music and the table was all set for breakfast.

Humming along with the radio, Stan slotted two slices of bread in the toaster. Through the window he could see his father ambling up the garden, still chatting away over the fence. Above him, he could hear sounds of Floella beginning to stir.

He opened the apricot jam, waggling his head in time to the music. It was nice to be somewhere new, even if it had been sad to leave Molehill Road. Today a bit of exploring could well be in order.

Pdung! The toast popped up.

Whistling Stan waltzed over to the toaster and whipped the hot toast out. Then he twirled towards the table.

And froze.

The paper... the *Riverditch News*... was lying on the table. And a face stared up at him out of the front page. A face he recognized.

Stan's legs began to shake. His heart began to pound. But not just because of the photograph. It was the word in big black type below it that really made Stan's head start to swim.

MISSING

Local boy genius disappears

Fears are growing for the safety of eleven year old Raymond Golightly, who has been missing since early yesterday afternoon.

He was last seen by his parents, Daphne and Marcus Golightly, getting off a number 22 bus bound for Glade Park. He had spent the morning at the Riverditch Museum for the opening of the new Outer Space Exhibition. Mrs Golightly, the eminent quantum physicist, had given a most interesting talk entitled *Theories of Gravity*.

It seems Raymond and his parents all boarded the bus together bound for their home in Parkside Rise. But as the bus was approaching Glade Hill, Raymond suddenly changed his plans. He asked if he could stop off at the hardware store in Glade Hill Parade, as there was something he had to buy for his latest project.

"We saw no harm in it," said his father. "The Parade is only a couple of stops before ours, and we know how keen he is always to get on with things."

"That was the last we saw of him," said a tearful Mrs. Golightly. "It was just after two o'clock – I remember because of Raymond's watch. He's programmed it to play three bars of a Bach Cantata on the hour. It went off just before he got off the bus."

Where Raymond went after he left the bus is a mystery. He never visited the hardware store, nor any of the other shops in Glade Hill Parade. And he never came home.

So far the Police are refusing to make any connection between this and earlier unsolved disappearances in the area. "We see no reason to link this case with any other at this stage," said Inspector Bland, heading the enquiry. "It would be fair to say, however, that we keep an open mind on these matters."

Raymond's parents are appealing for help from the public. "It is most unlike Ray not to contact us," said his father. "He is such a home bird."

Brainy Raymond is something of a recent local celebrity. Only last month he was the winner of the hotly contested Riverditch Science Superbrain competition, open to everyone under 15. Entrants were invited to submit projects based on their own, original studies of the local area.

Raymond was the runaway winner with his comparative study of rainfall, humidity and agricultural productivity in Riverditch and its twin town in France, Petitfosse.

6

MISSING

Trembling, Stan sat down. A voice kept saying the same thing over and over again in his head. *It can't be true. It can't be true.*

His hands clenched the table until his knuckles turned white. It was like a dream, a bad dream... except it was real. And there, slapped right across the front page of the *Riverditch News* was the photograph to prove it. A great big photograph of the very same face Stan had seen staring out of the window of the weird old house beyond the trees. The face of Raymond Golightly, the boy who was missing.

"What's up?" yawned Floella, slopping into the kitchen. "You look all peaky. Sort of shivery looking."

Stan couldn't speak, couldn't say a word. He couldn't make sense of a thing. His hand was trembling as it clutched the corner of the paper.

Floella snatched it out of his hands. "Goofball Golightly!" she said gaping down at the paper. "What's *he* doing on the front page?"

"Wow," she breathed, seeing the headline. "Well, he might have beaten us to the Science Superbrain prize, but this..." She shook her head and started reading.

Of course. Now Stan remembered. Floella and her friend Margery had been up for the Science Superbrain prize too. Not that it mattered.

"Floella..." he said, tugging at her sleeve.

"Weeks we spent making our working model of the sewage plant," said Floella, head down, still scanning the page.

"I've seen him, Floella," said Stan, tugging harder. "I saw him yesterday. At a window."

Floella was still reading, looking shocked now. "Poor old Ray," she said. "He wasn't so bad, really. He almost deserved to win. Almost."

Stan got up. He had to tell her, make her listen. He grabbed her shoulders. "I saw a face at a window, Floella," he said. "It was *his*!"

Floella looked at him blankly. She didn't have a clue what he was talking about. Stan slumped down next to her. It was clear he was going to have to tell her the whole thing.

He did his best, but he could tell from the look on her face that Floella didn't believe a word of it.

"I know it sounds ridiculous," he said as he finally ground to a halt. "I can't explain it..."

"I can," said Floella suddenly. "There's a perfectly simple explanation." Then she stared hard at him, with an irritating fake smile on her face. "You're making it up," she said.

"I'm not..." Stan began to protest.

But she hadn't finished. She held up her hand. "Let me get this right," she said. "You say you saw this face at the window of that empty old house."

She went to the window. "That one over there, up the hill a bit, through the trees," she said, pointing. "Lots of windows and turrety bits?"

Stan nodded miserably.

Floella narrowed her eyes. "Approximate distance..." she paused and frowned as if she was doing some sort of complicated sum in her head... "twice as long as a football pitch. More or less."

"Then this face vanished. Whoosh! Just like that?" she continued. "And it was the face of Raymond Golightly, who is now missing."

Stan dropped his head into his hands. He shouldn't have told her. Put this way, he didn't believe his story either.

"Stan," said Floella, looking horribly smug. "It's another of your stories isn't it?" Now she was tapping her fingers on the table. "But you can't get me to believe *this* one. No one would. It's pathetic."

"You're losing your touch," she continued. "It's not nearly as scary as the ghost in the wardrobe. And it's stupider than the one about the toenail snatcher under my bed."

It was useless. He should have known it would be. She didn't believe a word of it. And she hadn't finished yet.

"Besides which, you couldn't possibly have seen a face so clearly from that distance."

"I know," said Stan miserably. "But I did."

"Oh really," said Floella, leaning forward. "Well, explain this. When did you say you saw this face?"

"Twelve o'clock," said Stan. "I'd just looked at my watch."

"Hah!" shouted Floella. "Caught you out! Read it again," she continued relentlessly, jabbing at the paper. "He didn't go missing until two. See. You couldn't have seen him."

Case proved, Floella paused for breath. Then she frowned. "It's not something to make things up about, you know," she said. "He is missing after all. It's not that funny, Stan."

"But this isn't a joke," said Stan, despairing. "I'm *not* making it up. There was a face at the window and it was the same as the face in that photo. I'm sure of it."

7

CRUSHER

Half an hour later Stan wasn't so sure. He was slouching on the front door step drawing faces in the gravel with a long stick. Maybe Floella was right. Perhaps he hadn't *really* seen the face. It might be just his imagination, making something out of nothing.

Crrrrrk. Crrrrrk. He looked up.

The garage door was opening. Floella was coming out wheeling her bike. She had a big plastic bucket looped over one handlebar. Dad's favourite tea towel was covering the top so Stan couldn't see what was inside it, but both Floella's hands were stained blue.

"This time I'll get it right," she announced,

pushing her notebook into her saddlebag. "But just in case, I shall be carrying out further trials at a secret location." With that, she leapt onto her bike.

"Time is of the essence," she called over her shoulder as she pedalled purposefully to the junction at the bottom of The Glades.

Stan watched her from his seat on the front doorstep until she disappeared round the corner into the main road. He stood up.

And that was when his insides turned a double somersault. "N-ooo," breathed Stan. "It can't be." But there was no doubt.

Cycling up The Glades was a horrible sight. Six foot of smirking muscles and grease: Colin 'Crusher' Armitage. Pushing fifteen and mean as they come.

Crusher considered himself something of a local celebrity. He had just won a Mr. Muscles competition – walked it really. In a few short hours he had demolished the opposition, and lifted the weight of an average six-year-old more than his nearest rival, or so he said.

He had been featured on local TV, interviewed on the radio and had made the front page of the *Riverditch News*.

And right now he was cycling up Stan's road, getting nearer and nearer.

Stan shuddered. Crusher was about the last person in the world he wanted to see. He could remember their last meeting all too clearly. It had started with a play rehearsal and an insult that somehow just popped out of Stan's mouth...

..."Good morning, Baa-lamb Lambkin," Crusher had said with a snigger, blocking the school gate. "Care to lend me your pocket money?"

Stan padlocked his bike to the railings and walked firmly towards the gate.

"Good morning, Colin," he said. "Learnt your line yet?"

Crusher's jaw dropped. Too late, Stan came back to earth with a bump. What on earth had he done? Two insults at once. He'd pay for that, all right.

For starters, he'd used Crusher's real name. Crusher loathed it. Well, it was hardly the sort of name to strike terror into the hearts of small boys and girls...

Then there was the matter of Crusher's lines – a delicate subject. It wasn't that Crusher had wanted to be in the play. He was more forced into it.

But once in the play, he wanted the biggest part and, sadly, Crusher couldn't act. He could sing, though. He could sing like an angel.

Inside that strapping great hulk was a voice that made children beg to give their toys to the needy, that made brothers love sisters and teachers love pupils. Even Blodgett had been known to dab at his eyes when Crusher sang.

But he couldn't act.

So week after week, hefty great chunks had been cut out of his part until there was almost nothing left except songs. Crusher was a little sensitive about it.

Which probably explained why he was now brick-red and hopping mad. "You're in serious trouble, Stan-ley," he hissed, grabbing Stan by the collar.

Stan agreed. He held his breath.

Putt-putt, VROOOM!

In the nick of time, Mr. Platt, writer, producer and director of the school play, zoomed through the gates on his yellow moped and screeched to a halt. "Rehearsal starts now!" he beamed, beckoning them into the school hall.

Stan breathed again. Saved. For the time being, anyway.

But the rehearsal had ended abruptly a few minutes later, halfway through the big number – just after Crusher got to pick up Melanie Gubbins and twirl her around his head.

Alas for the unfortunate Melanie, heartbreakingly lovely star of the play, Crusher lost his grip on her. She shot out of his arms and onto a half-painted piece of balcony scenery.

Sadly, it was also only half-built.

Within seconds, the whole thing had collapsed and a wailing Melanie Gubbins disappeared under a heap of cardboard and plywood. All you could see was a little bit of her floaty blue frock flapping forlornly on the balcony railings – or what was left of them. Mr. Platt called a halt to rehearsals and promptly whisked her off to casualty.

After that, Stan slunk off as fast as he could. It was only a matter of time before Crusher would remember the unfinished business he still had with Stan. As he left, he could hear Crusher, proud and excited, reliving the glory of the moment when Melanie Gubbins shot skywards.

"Bruises big as saucers she'll have. Just like the time when little Wilson asked me to help get his kite out of the oak tree. Well, I chucked him up the tree as far as I could but somehow, he missed the branch. Couldn't even eat the grapes I brought him in hospital."

Then something struck Crusher.

"Talking of hospital, where's Lampkin? By the time I've finished with him, he'll wish..."

Stan didn't hang around to hear any more...

Yes, that had been the last time Stan and Crusher had met. And now, here he was, pedalling up Stan's road, casual as you please. Then he stopped, got off his bike and took out a key.

Stan's heart lurched. What a prospect. It was a thought too horrible to contemplate, but Crusher was behaving with every appearance of someone who might well live in that house. Number 32.

SLAM!

The front door of number 40 banged shut behind Stan, caught by a freak gust of wind. Stan moaned. How unlucky could you get?

Crusher looked up. He saw Stan and a ghastly grin spread slowly across his face. He shook his head, put his keys back in his pocket and started to swagger up the road.

Stan's heart was pumping away like a road drill. Floella was out. Dad was out. And Crusher didn't look as if he was planning a welcome party.

Stan had to get out of here. Fast.

He charged through the side gate and slammed it behind him. He pelted down the side passage into the back garden.

Hide! a voice was saying in his head. *Hide! Before it's too late!*

8

GETAWAY

"Stanley, Stanley Lampkin. I'll find you, wherever you are."

Stan ran down the garden at full pelt. His breath came in great aching gasps with every stride. At the bottom of the garden he slumped against the wooden fence. There was nowhere to hide. Nowhere. Crusher would find him in seconds.

Unless...

He looked up. The fence was high but he might just make it and there must be a million places to hide in all those trees on the other side. Crusher would never find him there.

Stan jumped and caught hold of the splintery top of the fence. Then he grabbed the branch of an old tree which hung over from the other side. Grunting with effort, he pulled his legs up onto the fence, took a deep breath, shut his eyes and jumped.

In the nick of time.

The creak of a hinge told him Crusher had just opened the side gate into the garden. Stan crouched down against the fence, hardly daring to breathe.

"I'll get you Stanley. If not today, another time," promised a gloating voice, thick with menace.

Now Stan could hear the steady thud, thud, thud of Crusher's feet lumbering down the garden. He could almost see that big stupid face, eyes glittering, searching left and right for some sign of his prey.

How long would it take before he worked out where Stan had gone?

Stan scrambled to his feet. He started to run, Dead branches snapped left and right under his trainers as he shot away as fast as he could. There was some sort of path, covered in dead leaves and overgrown with wild trailing creepers. He followed it deeper into the tangled woods, thinking only of escape, not stopping to wonder where it might lead.

He ran gasping for breath. He couldn't stop. Not yet. Not while there was a chance that Crusher would find him.

The path curved suddenly to the right, but straight ahead of him was an old iron gate. Was there somewhere to hide through there? Somewhere beyond the path? There *had* to be.

Stan rattled at the gate, harder and harder. He could hear the thud thud thud of Crusher's feet pounding down the path now. *"Open,"* Stan begged the gate. *"Please open."* It was no use. It wouldn't budge. He scrambled over the top and dived for the cover of the tall dark trees beyond.

Crusher's cries grew fainter, but still Stan didn't dare stop. He ran blindly on along a rough overgrown track through the dense wood.

Sobbing with exhaustion he glanced back over his shoulder, just to make sure...

CRASH!

He ran smack bang into something rock-hard at full speed. Winded, he fell to the ground and lay there, face-down in the undergrowth.

Great shuddering gasps forced their way, one after another, from his mouth. He struggled to control them. He mustn't *mustn't* let Crusher know where he was.

But Crusher was nowhere to be seen. Not a sound of him either. Had Crusher given up the chase, or was it a trick?

Stan waited – and waited – to be absolutely sure. Still there was silence. At last he sat up wiping his sleeve across his face. He blinked. Now he could see what had sent him crashing to the ground.

A great stone slab, half-hidden by creepers and

covered in moss. It looked a bit like a gravestone. Stan shivered. It was an odd place for one. There was an inscription carved into one side. The letters were clear, no moss or creepers, nothing grew over them to obscure the strange words:

AND THOSE WHO DISCOVER
FEAR BEYOND FEAR
SHALL BE LOST FOREVER
CAST IN STONE

Stan rubbed at his eyes again. Beyond the slab, at the very edge of the wood, was a figure, a statue. It seemed to be pointing.

Stan walked towards it, slowly, a little hesitantly. Of course, he thought. I should have realized. This is the garden... the garden of the old house.

The statue was of a man, carved out of smooth, grey stone. A huge figure, a giant of a man. It had its back to him, but the face was turned to one side, neck bent back, mouth stretched wide. One arm was bent, clenched, as if in pain. The other was outstretched and pointing. Pointing into the garden. Pointing towards a mass of other human figures.

A mass of statues cast in cold, grey stone.

Stan stared, then stumbled towards them until he was surrounded. Surrounded by a crowd of petrified figures, some standing, some sitting, some cowering, bent and twisted. Stone statues of people – men and women, children too – different ages, different types. Lifesize and so lifelike that Stan instinctively reached out to touch one, as if to check...

It was cold. Colder than cold, like ice under his fingers.

But it was the faces that shocked Stan.

Faces of terror. Faces twisted into the most terrible expressions of fear. And something else as well. Hate. Hate and fear.

Stan didn't want to look, didn't want to see any more. But there was something about those statues... He couldn't tear his eyes away from them.

It was as if every single one had been captured in stone at the moment of seeing something so terrible, so horrible, that all other thoughts, all reason, had been driven away.

Leaving only terror. Sheer terror.

They were hideous. Arms thrown up, bodies arched backwards, mouths contorted into silent screams of despair. "They're so real," whispered Stan. "So real..."

And beyond, beyond the statues and the neglected garden was the old dark house. Standing silent and sinister, like some gigantic monster carved out of stone, with every window tightly shuttered against the daylight. Every window that is, except one. High up, just under the eaves, a single arched window stared out.

Get away from here, said a voice in Stan's head. *Get away from here before something happens. Something beyond your control. Now!*

But Stan couldn't turn away. He was powerless to turn and run.

The statues, the shuttered windows, the looming house... this place was unnatural. Even the air felt thick and heavy with menace. Something was wrong, Stan could feel it. And he could feel something else. A presence... a presence of evil.

Go now!

Stan tried to turn away, willing his legs to move, to run, to escape. He stumbled backwards, still unable to turn his head away. Backwards across the long grass, away from the house and the statues, back towards the safety of the wood and the trees.

Then he turned on his heels and ran, faster and faster still, until he came to the old iron gate where he stopped dead in his tracks. He screamed.

9

CONVERSATIONS

Something had hold of him. Something small and growly, with a lot of fur and sharp teeth.

"Towser!" came a sharp cry from somewhere beyond the bushes. "Drop!"

The effect was immediate. Towser – as the small furry thing attached to Stan's left trainer was presumably known – dropped. Then he hung his head.

"I'm so sorry," called the voice. "You startled him. He's never seen anyone in there before."

Stan looked up to see a figure hurrying down the footpath in the woods towards him. Someone about as old as Dad, with a hole in the knee of her trousers and a seed packet sticking out of her pocket.

Stan climbed over the gate. More slowly than before, but with his heart still beating away in double quick time.

"I know who you are," said the person, panting slightly, while Towser slobbered all over her ankles. "You're Stan. Your dad showed me a photo of you."

She held out her hand. "I'm Imelda. From number 42." Stan had never felt so grateful to a neighbour before – mentioner or not. Not that she looked much like a mentioner.

Imelda led Stan back along the footpath through the woods. It weaved its way towards the fence at the bottom of his garden. He could see a broken branch lying on a trampled, muddy patch of grass. Funny. He didn't remember breaking that branch...

No he *hadn't* broken that branch. No prizes for guessing who had. Stan shuddered. Wherever Crusher was now, one thing was certain. He'd be back.

The path swung round and skirted along below the fence, below the stone wall at the bottom of Imelda's garden and up round the side.

"It's a public right of way," Imelda said as they walked. "Not that many people use it. I only do because of Towser. Those woods aren't exactly a beauty spot. And as for the house..."

"Who lives there?" asked Stan, suddenly.

Imelda looked surprised. "No one. It's empty,

in a terrible state. It's just been left all these years and..."

"Who owns it then?" Stan interrupted.

"Now? Who knows," Imelda shrugged. "It used to belong to a doctor... a surgeon, I think." She frowned. "I only met him once. That was enough."

They had reached the top of the path now and a tall wooden gate barred their way. Imelda undid the latch and opened the gate, ushering Stan through ahead of her. To Stan's surprise, they were back in The Glades, right beside the house at the end – Imelda's house.

"Helloooo!"

Floella suddenly swept round the corner into The Glades, screeched to a halt and leapt off her bike. She still had the bucket looped over one handlebar, only now there was a gaping hole in it.

"I may well be on the verge of an exciting new breakthrough," she gasped triumphantly, plonking the bucket on the ground. "Another day or two of trials should do it."

There were blobs of something bright blue all over Floella's leggings – whatever it was, it sent Towser into a frenzy – and her feet and ankles were coated in wet, slimy mud.

Imelda was gaping at Floella. She looked in danger of forgetting her conversation with Stan. She might, but Stan wasn't going to. "So this doctor..." he said.

"Oh him," said Imelda. "There were all sorts of rumours about him... about the work he did in that house, strange goings on, things like that. He was a very arrogant sort of man, secretive too. And downright rude. People didn't like him, didn't trust him, and so the stories began to spread. To tell the truth I didn't take much notice. Then he left."

"Left?" said Stan.

"Went away. Disappeared. Died. Who knows?" said Imelda. "I think there was some sort of trouble, something serious, a scandal. Whatever it was, the house was suddenly empty. One day he was there, the next he was gone. The place was just shut up. The doors were bolted, the windows were shuttered and that was that. He's never been seen since."

"So the house is still empty?" said Stan.

Imelda nodded. "Totally. No one ever goes there, not even the postman. I shouldn't think anyone has been through the front gate or up the drive in years." She paused and gave Stan, a secret, knowing sort of grin. "Of course you can get into the garden from the back, through the woods, through that iron gate where I met you... but not many people know that."

She turned to go. "It's a crime to let that garden go." she said. "I could do without those statues, mind, but the shrubs are magnificent." She shook her head. "I took a few cuttings last year. I shouldn't have, but I didn't think anyone would mind." She went through the front gate into number 42. "Sad thing was," she added as she shut the gate, "every single one of them died..."

With a wave she was gone. Then Floella shot off and Stan was left alone on the kerb, thinking about the house and its neglected garden, and the grey stone statues.

Back inside the house, it was clear that Dad had been shopping again, judging by the plastic carrier bags littering the floor. He was clutching some seed packets in one hand and a big round package in the other. He handed it to Stan. "Open it," he said, with a grin.

Stan attacked the parcel with the kitchen scissors. A dartboard! He'd been going on at Dad about getting a dartboard for ages. He'd even offered to give up his monthly horror magazine for one. But Dad had always gone on about darts being dangerous.

"Wow, thanks Dad, it's brilliant..." Stan started to say.

Dad looked straight at him. "We'll make this a real home again, Stan," his Dad said, "I promise." Then he smiled.

Stan nodded. He knew what his father was trying to say.

How long had it been now? Nearly three years, but Stan could remember that day as if it was only last week. He remembered the big emptiness that had reached out and swallowed them all up whole.

It had been a Tuesday, the day his mother died. A bright sunny day. Stan remembered how strange it had seemed, hearing all that laughter from the children in the school playground up the road.

In their house there hadn't been a sound. Even the old wind-up clock in the hall had stopped ticking. Winding it had always been something his mother did.

The three of them were there, but still the house had felt empty.

And silent.

The silence had gone on for days, weeks, even months after that.

Stan had tiptoed around, puzzled by it all, not quite knowing what to do. Not quite understanding anything. There had been no one to talk to. No one. No one to ask about things – like why she got ill, why she couldn't get better, and why she had to go and die.

Floella had buried herself in her books. Maybe it had been worse for her, she was older and understood more. But it was hard to tell with Floella. She never talked about it. She'd probably filed her feelings under Grief in her *Human Behaviour* notebook.

And Dad... Dad did everything he was supposed to do. He ferried them about, to school, to friends' houses, on shopping trips. He even sometimes got as far as mentioning Mum.

But always in that voice, the jolly one, the one packed with false cheer. The voice he used for persuading Stan to do something like swallowing vile medicine or visiting Great-Uncle Archie. His 'this-won't-hurt-a-bit' voice. It did, though.

It had gone on like that for a long time. A horribly long time. But things were getting better now, much better in fact, ever since that day last summer when Dad got out a big box packed with photos.

Stan and Floella had never seen them before. There were pictures of them as babies and small children – laughing, happy photos with their mother and father. All of them together.

Then Dad had put his arm round Stan and said, "You look like her, you know." He had said it in a perfectly normal voice. Not sad, not happy, not pretend bright and cheery, just normal.

And Floella had sat there, staring down at one of the photos, clutching it so tightly it started to curl up in her hand.

"It was the worst day of my life," she had said suddenly. Then she had bawled her eyes out. So had Dad.

Stan had watched, almost shocked. He had never seen Floella cry before. Or Dad, come to that. Not that way, not without pretending it was a cold, or itchy eyes or something.

Somehow, after that, things started to get better. The move was the next big step – leaving the past behind – not forgetting it, but not *living* in it...

Stan chose the spot for the dartboard. Floella put it up. And after that they had a brilliant evening, talking and laughing and sorting through all the photos again.

Dad asked Floella and Stan to help him choose one of their mother to put on the mantelpiece above the fireplace.

They pored over the possibilities. In the end they settled for one of her in a flowery bikini, with Stan and Floella crawling on top of her, both wearing floppy yellow sunhats.

Then Dad sizzled some big fat sausages in a pan until they were brown and burst and crunchy, cooked just right. They ate every scrap.

Yes, it was a brilliant evening – until they turned on the TV.

10

IN THE NIGHT

"And now, we interrupt the evening's viewing for a local newsflash." Even before the photo was flashed up on the screen Stan knew what it would be about.

Raymond Golightly was still missing.

The police were baffled. There were no clues to his disappearance, no sightings and no leads to his whereabouts. They were appealing to anyone with any information to come forward.

Anyone with any information...

That meant Stan. Or did it? He had seen something that he couldn't possibly have seen. What kind of information was that?

How *could* he go to the police? What would he

say? That he'd seen a face in the window of an empty house? That the face belonged to the boy who later went missing? That the house was way beyond the woods at the end of the garden, a hundred yards away at least... yet he could see the face clearly?

No. *None* of it was possible. If Floella had laughed at him, what would the police do?

And Dad. What would he think? He could picture Dad's face as he came out with his 'information'. Dad would look all grave and serious. "This is not a time for stories, Stan," he would say. "It's important that you tell the truth."

He could see them leaving the police station, total disappointment written all over his Dad's face. And that would be the worst thing of all.

Well, why *should* Dad believe his story? Stan hardly believed it himself.

The house was empty. Imelda said so and she should know. He'd been there himself, well, the garden anyway. All right so it had been a bit scary, but the place was deserted. Not a sign of life anywhere.

So there couldn't have been anyone at the window and even if there had been, he couldn't have seen them from his bedroom. It was too far away. And it couldn't have been Raymond, because he was somewhere else at the time.

He had imagined it. He must have done.

Even so, he couldn't forget that face, the way it seemed to look at him, those empty staring eyes, so lifelike, yet so lifeless.

Miserably, Stan trailed off to bed. He pulled the duvet up to his chin and lay there, his head turned away from the window. If only Dad had got him some curtains...

He heard Floella go upstairs, then later, Dad taking the stairs three at a time, humming to himself. He heard him run a bath, then potter round his bedroom. He heard the click of a light switch. Dad had gone to bed.

The whole house was in darkness. The sounds of the evening gave way to the silence of the night. It made no difference. Stan couldn't sleep.

Outside, the jagged black outline of the old house stretched up into the moonlight. Huge, threatening and deserted. Yes, deserted. Imelda had said so.

Stan shut his eyes tight. He wouldn't look at the house. He wouldn't even think about it, not for a second.

But it was still out there. He knew it was. Even with his eyes shut tight, he could see the lone arched window and the face that stared straight at him, straight through him, with that blank, blank gaze... Raymond Golightly, still missing.

He leapt out of bed. He *had* to tell Dad, whatever his reaction. He had to tell Dad about all the things going round in his head. Maybe he would have an answer, at least tell him he wasn't going mad. Tell him *something*, help him to understand.

He crept along the passage. Quietly, he opened the door to Dad's room and crept over to the bed.

"Dad," he whispered. There was no reply.

"Dad," he tried again, a bit louder this time. Still no reply.

He stood looking down. His father was fast asleep. Stan put out a hand to touch his shoulder. Dad stirred, then rolled over and away from Stan.

Stan took his hand away. He couldn't do it. He couldn't wake him. He couldn't begin to explain.

Help me, whispered a voice in his head. *Please help me. I don't know what to do.* But he didn't try to wake Dad again.

Back in his bed, he clung onto his pillow. He had never felt so alone, not since Mum's death. Never.

And when at last he slept, he fell into a strange and fearful dream. It was a dream that made him cry out in terror, a dream where someone held out their arms towards him, pleading for help. The face was in shadow. All Stan could see were outstretched arms and eyes, panic-stricken eyes, staring straight at him.

He could hear a voice whispering again and again in his ear, *"Help me. Help me, before it's too late."*

"Who are you?" Stan shouted over and over, tossing and turning in his bed. "Who are you?"

But there was no answer. The eyes disappeared, the voice faded away.

All that was left was the sound of laughter. Evil laughter, cruel laughter, great howls of laughter that made him cry out with fear.

He woke, terrified. He sat bolt upright, sweating and clutching the bedclothes close to his chest. The sound of laughter was still ringing in his ears.

"Go away!" he screamed, shaking his head from side to side, still half-asleep. "Leave me alone!"

He looked at the clock... one thirty. Was that all? Hours and hours of the night still to get through. Hours and hours of darkness. Hours and hours all alone.

He stumbled out of his bed and stood in the middle of the floor, shaking and breathing deep breaths until he was properly awake. Wide awake.

Then he turned round. He looked out through the curtainless window, out beyond the woods to the old house. There *was* something there. Something at that lone arched window.

A face, blank and expressionless, eerie in its absolute stillness. A face that seemed to glow, as if it were lit from the inside by a cold, bright light. A face with pale luminous skin, and shining staring eyes. A face clear in every detail. So clear that it seemed larger than life.

"N-n-n-no," moaned Stan. He didn't want to look, didn't want to see, but he couldn't tear his eyes away.

The face was looking straight out... but it wasn't the pale, ghostly face of Raymond Golightly. It was someone quite different. Someone he had seen only yesterday.

But this time there was no sneer. No smirk. No curl of the lip. None of the things usually found on the face of Colin 'Crusher' Armitage.

Just a blank, blank face. Expressionless, just like the face of Raymond Golightly had been.

Don't let this be happening, begged a voice in Stan's head. *It can't be. Please don't let this be happening.*

He tried to move towards the door. He had to get away, get away from the window and out of the room. It was no good. His legs wouldn't support him.

He fell to the floor.

11

DARK DAY

Floella found him in the same spot, slumped on the floor, early the next morning.

"Wake up, Stan! Wake up."

Floella was tugging at the sleeve of Stan's pyjamas. He looked up at her, confused, bewildered and stiff with cold. What was he doing on the floor? Then he remembered.

"I saw it again. A face. Only this time it was Crusher. At the window. Just staring. I saw it again! Not Raymond Golightly, but Crusher."

He was clutching onto Floella's arm. He couldn't stop the words pouring out, tumbling over each other, all jumbled up. But it didn't matter, so long as he could make her understand.

"The face – it looked right through me, just like before. Larger than life – it was Crusher, clear as clear. I could see him, sort of glowing at the window and in my dream there was this voice..."

He wiped his face and took a deep breath. Then he looked at Floella. What was she going to do? Laugh? Tell him he was crazy? Fetch Dad?

She did none of those things.

"Hmmm," she said.

Is that it? thought Stan. No more?

"Another face?" Floella said. "And this time it was Crusher's." She sat, deep in thought. "Most interesting," she continued.

Stan slammed his fist hard onto the floor. "It's not interesting!" he screamed. "It's terrifying! And it's true, every single word of it!"

"I believe you," said Floella.

He slumped on the floor with relief.

"At least," she added. "I believe that *you* believe it's true."

"Floella," he said through gritted teeth. "I am not making this up, you know."

"That's what you *think,*" said Floella. A horribly patient and understanding note had crept into her voice. "But that doesn't mean it's actually true."

"It's amazing how the human brain can react under stress," she added, staring at him as if he were a newly discovered species. "It's understandable of course, a natural reaction, what with the move, new things to get used to and everything being different."

"But I'm not..." Stan began to protest. This was hopeless.

Floella stood up. She was ready to expand on her diagnosis. "Believe me, you're suffering from some form of self-induced delusion, Stan. It's obvious," she said. "Brought about by the current dramatic changes taking place in your circumstances."

She looked rather proud of herself. And what was worse, she looked as if she wanted to be helpful. "You're worried about Crusher. I know that, but we can sort him out. You didn't want to leave Molehill Road, but..."

If he listened to any more of this, Stan thought he might hit her... "I saw Crusher, Floella," he said. "I really, really saw him – with my own eyes. I know I did. I saw his fat ugly face staring at me from that window. I saw every eyelash, every detail, even that bulgy pimple on his chin."

Floella shook her head. "How? How could you see him so clearly? There's no way. It's too far away and it was the middle of the night. It was dark! Look, you can't even see that big plant pot through the shed window – and that's only at the end of the garden."

Stan felt like crying. Nothing he said would convince her. She was never going to believe him.

Nor would Dad. Nor would anyone. He couldn't have seen what he'd seen. It was impossible. *But*, whispered a voice in his head, *it happened. Somehow.*

"There is of course one other possibility," she said, standing up to leave the room. Stan looked up. "It could be that fifth sausage you ate last night. Maybe that's what did it." Then she went downstairs to breakfast.

The day got worse after that. Stan tried to convince himself that Floella was right, that it was just his imagination working overtime, making something out of nothing. He tried to convince himself, he *wanted* to convince himself, but it was hard.

All day his mind kept returning to the faces, to the old house beyond the trees, with its dark shuttered windows and its garden full of screaming statues. *Was* there something going on inside that empty house? Something that couldn't be explained away by common sense?

The harder he tried *not* to think these thoughts, the harder it became to get them out of his mind. He had to keep busy, concentrate on other things.

He followed his father from room to room with offers of help. He didn't want to be alone, not for a moment. He scoured the kitchen sink, he scrubbed the floor, he polished the tiles until they gleamed. He swept the cellar as if his life depended on it.

Anything to stop him thinking.

He tried phoning Midge, but there was no reply, even the answer machine was off. There was no one else he wanted to see right now. No one he could explain things to. So he did his piano practice, nearly an hour of it. Scale after scale at breakneck speed until he thought his fingers would drop off.

That was when Dad stepped in. "Where does it hurt?" he asked, looking all anxious and feeling Stan's forehead for signs of fever.

"Nowhere," said Stan miserably. He couldn't begin to tell his father the problem.

He wandered off to clean out the guinea pig's hutch, but those two blank faces were with him. Nothing blocked out the image of the way they had looked – so still, like a frozen moment of time, and so clear, so very clear.

No, whatever he did, wherever he went, the house was still out there. It's waiting, thought Stan uneasily. It's waiting for something.

At last, the longest day of Stan's life drew to a close and the light began to fade. Stan pulled the downstairs curtains, glad to shut out the sight of the trees and the chimney tops of the old house.

Sitting down by the fire, he watched the little gas flames leaping around the mock lumps of coal. He shivered. *Something awful is about to happen,* said the small voice inside his head. Don't be ridiculous, he tried to answer back.

But the idea stayed there, nagging at him, niggling its way into every other thought. Something awful was about to happen, something wrong, something evil...

"What's up with you?" Floella said coming into the room. "Still seeing visions?" And she gave a little smirk.

Stan swallowed hard. It wasn't funny. He was terrified. "They weren't visions, Floella. I saw them. I saw Raymond, then I saw Crusher. I'm not making it up," he said wretchedly.

Floella chewed on the end of a pencil. "What happens next then?" she asked in a sickly sweet voice. "Does Crusher disappear too?"

Stan bit his lip. Hot tears were pricking at the back of his eyes.

Rat, tat, tat. Someone rapped the front door knocker smartly up and down three times. Floella jumped up and looked at Stan.

"Visitors? At this time of night?" said Dad coming out of the kitchen with a pair of newly polished shoes in his hand. Floella followed him to the front door.

Seconds later she was back in the sitting room. She had bright pink circles in the middle of her cheeks and a strange glittery look in her eyes. "Errm... It's the police..." she said. She seemed to be having difficulty getting her words out.

Behind her lumbered two police officers and

Dad. "Sorry to bother you so late," said the burlier of the two.

"Not at all," said Dad, gesturing towards the armchairs by the fire. "What can I do for you?"

"We're conducting house to house enquiries, sir," said the burly one, easing himself into a chair. "A missing person's enquiry. A lad of fourteen disappeared overnight. Lives in this street. Name of Colin Armitage."

12

WHAT NOW?

The front door slammed shut. The policemen were gone.

"Wow," breathed Floella. "Amazing." She dragged Stan upstairs and into his bedroom, sat him down on the bed and looked at him with awe. "You're psychic, that's what it is," she said.

She jiggled from foot to foot with excitement. After all, what else could it be? He had told her about Crusher's face at the window long before he knew Crusher had disappeared.

"You're having premonitions, seeing into the future," she went on, eyes gleaming. "Those faces – they're some kind of projections from your imagination. Extra-sensory visions even. You're homing in on invisible waves in the atmosphere, invisible time lines linked to the future..."

Floella could call it what she liked, Stan didn't care. She was wrong. He knew what he'd seen.

"I should have told them," he said, miserably punching the pillow. "I should have told the police about the faces. Made them go and investigate the house."

He sat silent and brooding. He hadn't told the police a thing. When it came to the crunch he just couldn't. He had opened his mouth to speak but nothing came out.

They had all been sitting in a group looking so solemn and serious, so very... well, grown up. He knew, he just knew, they would never believe an impossible story about faces at the window.

The front door slammed again. Dad was off to a welcome party at Imelda's. He'd be out for a few hours, at least.

Stan hugged his pillow. The light beside his bed threw a warm glow onto the walls. It was beginning to feel like home, here in this house. Cosy and snug. Safe, even.

Not like outside.

Stan paced over to the window. Outside it was dark and stormy. The wind was howling round the garden and the rain was lashing down.

And outside that huge and silent house was towering up into the cloudy sky. It's waiting, thought Stan, without knowing why. Waiting for something. Or someone.

"Stan," said Floella. "Are you OK?"

He turned to face her. How long had he been standing by the window? It seemed like forever. She was sitting on the bed, watching him. She smiled at him.

Then the smile froze on her face. Only her eyes moved, travelled past him and looked outside. Her face turned white, white as a sheet. Every drop of blood drained from her face.

"What is it?" Stan said. "Floella, what's wrong?"

But she didn't answer. She just sat bolt upright, clutching onto the edge of the bed and staring out of the window.

"Stan," she whispered at last, as if she could hardly speak. "Oh Stan."

"What is it?" said Stan. He felt cold all over. His whole body felt frozen, cold as if his bones had been buried in ice. "Tell me!"

Then she spoke – whispered so quietly he could hardly hear her. "Look, Stan. Look out at the house. Look up at the window."

Stan couldn't move. He couldn't move but he had to. He had to look at the house, at the window – that tall arched window. Slowly, jerkily, he turned around and looked out.

There was a face at the window. He had known there would be. But not this one. Surely not this one.

He opened his mouth to speak but no words came out. There were no words to say.

There was a face there. Staring out at him from the window. Expressionless, blank and frozen in time. A face he knew well. Too well.

"Help me, Floella," croaked Stan. "Help me."

Floella clutched at his arm. Her knuckles were white. "That face," she whispered. "Oh Stan. Look at that face at the window. It's *you*."

13

THE OLD HOUSE

Then it was gone. One moment Stan's face stared blankly out from the window of the old house. The next, there was nothing there. Just the jagged outline of the old house against the night sky.

Stan stood still as a statue, rooted to the spot. He couldn't speak, he couldn't think, he couldn't even move a muscle. Then he began to shake uncontrollably, shivering as if he would never stop.

"Stan," said Floella quietly. "We have to do something."

She was still staring at the house, eyes fixed on the window. But even that was dark and indistinct now. There was nothing to be seen, not even the faintest flicker of light. Even so, she couldn't tear her eyes away.

"I'm scared, Floella," Stan whispered. "Scared to death. Raymond... Crusher... They're gone. And now it's my turn."

He hurled himself on the bed and buried his head in the pillow.

Floella stood silently for a moment, still staring out of the window into the darkness, staring at the still, dark shape of the old house. Then she turned away with a decisive nod.

"Follow me," she commanded, heading for the door. "We are going to sort this out!"

Stan shook his head and shrunk back on the bed. "What can we do?" he said. "We haven't got a clue what we're dealing with."

He had never felt so helpless in his life.

"Then we must find out!" said Floella grimly. "No one is going to make my little brother disappear. Not if I have anything to do with it."

Floella was back in control – but then, it hadn't been *her* face at the window.

"Wh-where are we going?" said Stan in a small voice. He knew full well what the answer would be.

"To that house, of course. And right now!"

Stan gulped. She was right. They had to do something. But not that. Anything but that.

"Couldn't we... maybe Dad?" he started to say.

"It won't work," said Floella flatly. "Can you

imagine it, waltzing into the party, asking him to go on some wild goose chase in the middle of a night like this?" She shook her head.

Still Stan didn't budge.

"Besides which, even if we did manage to persuade him, he's bound to say wait till the morning. We've got to act now," Floella urged. "We don't know how long we've got."

How long *I've* got, thought Stan, still not moving.

Floella looked at him, sitting there all scrunched up on the bed. He looked very small, all of a sudden, and frightened beyond belief. He was clutching his pillow as if he would never let it go.

"Look," she said, coming back over to him and sitting down. "We can't just sit here and wait." She handed him his jacket. "We won't stop it, whatever it is, by sitting here." She pulled him to his feet. "We have to go to the house."

She watched Stan put the jacket on.

"Ready?" she said.

Stan looked down at his feet.

"Ready," he said.

Outside the wind was whipping along The Glades. It was freezing cold and dark. Pitch dark. The moon had gone now and an army of black clouds had taken over every scrap of the sky.

"Floella," said Stan, standing shivering on the front doorstep. "Please. Let me speak to Dad first. Let me try."

Floella didn't say a word, just looked at him, then slowly nodded. Stan scurried up the path towards Imelda's front door. Hadn't Dad told Stan that he should always come to him with any problems? That nothing was too big to sort out between them?

On Imelda's doorstep, Stan hesitated. A little beam of light was shining out through a tiny chink in the curtain at the big, bay window. Maybe he'd just take a look first. He went right up close and peered in. There was Dad, over in the corner, talking to Imelda and someone else. He was laughing, looking happy, really happy, surrounded by people all dressed up in their posh clothes, all there to welcome him.

At least thirty of them, if not more.

Stan shrank back. He couldn't do it. He couldn't go in there. However much he wanted to, he couldn't just walk into that room full of people and embarrass Dad.

Nothing's too big... He could almost hear Dad's words ringing in his ears. But this one is, Dad, thought Stan. This one's too big. Then he turned and hurried away to where Floella was waiting.

Click. The gate to the woods swung open. They were through.

Heads down, Stan and Floella stumbled along the tangled path through the woods with only the thin beam of Floella's pocket torch to guide them along. Every stumbling step took them nearer and nearer the old house.

They were on the edge of the woods now. Hurrying, hurrying past the stone slab with its strange inscription, past the stone statues howling in their silent agony, across the overgrown garden, up a short flight of wide stone steps to the front of a door – huge, dark and forbidding.

Above them, the old house towered, silent as the grave. Deserted, not a sign of life behind any of those blank shuttered windows.

"Let's go," said Stan. His teeth were chattering so hard Floella could hardly hear the words he forced out. "Let's go home. Now."

Floella didn't budge. She caught hold of his arm. "Don't..."

She stopped. "Listen," she said.

They listened.

It was hard to tell above the noise of the wind, but Stan thought he could hear a noise, a sort of whining noise.

"What is it?" said Floella. "What's in there? Some kind of machine?"

Stan turned away. It was too much to take. "Floella," he said. "I can't."

Floella glared at him. "We have to get inside," she said.

Crrrk, crrrk.

Something was happening. Something was

moving. The vast oak door in front of them. They stood frozen as slowly, slowly the door swung open in front of their eyes. Not a bolt, not a chain, not a key. Nothing broke the silence but a mechanical whine and the creaking of unoiled hinges. And beyond the open door lay nothing. Just vast, empty blackness.

Floella stepped forward. Her expression looked set, utterly determined. Stan had never seen her look like that before.

Then she turned to Stan and smiled. "Stan," she said. "We'll get to the bottom of this. Trust me."

Brave words, but they didn't stop Stan shaking as he followed her inside.

14

NO TURNING BACK

Stan shivered. It was cold as a tomb inside the old house.

Their feet echoed in the silence as they tiptoed over the flagstones. That was the only sound except for the moan of the wind outside.

They were in a vast hallway. All around them dim shapes loomed out of the darkness, lit by the flickering beam of Floella's torch. The outline of a long table with empty chairs grouped around it, a grandfather clock with its hands frozen at midnight, an old stone fireplace with a carved inscription chiselled in the stone:

NO GLORY WITHOUT SACRIFICE

There were doors everywhere.

Doors to other dark shadowy rooms, thought Stan. Doors I don't want to open. Rooms I don't want to see.

He looked up. A row of portraits glowered down at him from the shadows.

This has never been a happy house, he thought. This house has never been filled with warmth, with laughter. You can just feel it. This is a house of gloom. A house of hate. Of evil.

And of danger.

But there was nothing here that might explain things. No Raymond. No Crusher. Only a voice in his head speaking over and over again. *Get out of here,* it warned. *Get as far away as you can. NOW.*

"Floella..." he said.

But Floella had already tiptoed away from him. She was standing in the middle of the vast stone hallway, listening.

"There's that noise again," she hissed. "What is it?"

It was a humming, thrumming noise, low and continuous... coming from somewhere up above. Somewhere far away at the top of the house.

Suddenly, they both froze. They could hear something else. Footsteps. Brisk footsteps tap-tap-tapping hurriedly across a room. A distant room.

And a laugh, not a merry laugh, not kind, not the laughter of a shared joke. But long and low and full of menace. A laugh that was coming from somewhere upstairs.

This was it. Whatever they were looking for, it was up there. Waiting... waiting for Stan.

Run, warned a voice in his head. *Run for it now, while you still can.*

Stan couldn't move. He looked at Floella.

"We have to go up there," she said quietly.

Stan shook his head. He couldn't. He couldn't go up there, not up that long dark staircase he could dimly make out across the hallway.

"It's the only way," whispered Floella. She took his hand.

Then they both crept towards the bottom of the staircase and began to climb. One hesitant step at a time, upstairs towards the humming noise and the footsteps and the laughter. But as they reached the top, the house was silent once more.

A dark, shadowy corridor lay ahead of them. A faint glimmer of light revealed a half open door at the far end. *This way,* it seemed to say, beckoning them on.

"I'm right beside you," whispered Floella, squeezing his hand.

Stan nodded, unable to speak.

Slowly they set off. Pace for pace, they matched each other along the corridor. Every footstep sounded loud as a thunderclap on the dusty floorboards.

Now they were outside the door. The faint, hopeful glimmer of light was gone.

I'm not going in there, thought Stan, but Floella stepped inside. Stan followed, unable to make his legs obey his mind.

They were standing in an enclosed space at the foot of a steep, stone staircase. A staircase that spiralled up into the darkness above. Floella began to climb. So did Stan. Slowly...

...Five more steps to the top.

Four.

Stan's feet felt like great lumps of concrete. It took every ounce of strength to move them.

Three.

The sound of that laugh – that horrible gloating, evil laugh – was echoing round his head.

Two.

It's not too late to turn back, a voice said in his head. *Not quite*. But deep in his heart, Stan knew that it was.

One.

None.

Straight ahead of them – just a step away – was another door, framed in an eerie glow of light. Dark, heavy, old... and shut.

Stan stood rooted to the spot. This was it. The moment had come. Whatever lay in store, he had to face it. He couldn't turn back now.

Don't go in there, screamed the voice in Stan's

head. *You may never come out again. NEVER!*

But it was too late. They watched as the door creaked slowly open.

"It looks like we're expected," said Floella, her face pale and expressionless.

Then they both stepped inside.

15

INTO DANGER

Of all the things Stan had imagined, nothing had prepared him for this. Nothing.

A bright, light room. Four bare walls lit by harsh white light that streamed down from spotlights in the ceiling. Under their glare, Floella's face turned into a cold, white mask as she looked at Stan and took a step inside.

Stan crept after her.

Apart from the sound of their feet on the bare wooden floor, the room was silent. And then the noise began again, the same low humming noise they had heard earlier, but louder, much louder. It was coming from a huge box made of dull grey metal in the centre of the room.

Stan stood and stared. Beside him, Floella did the same. "What is it?" she whispered. "What does it do?"

It was some sort of machine. Out of the back came a mass of wires and cables. Some were connected to an ordinary looking computer screen and keyboard. Others ran to plugs in the wall. But it was the thick red cable taped to the floor that really caught their attention. It led to what looked like some kind of giant telescope. A telescope pointing straight at a window.

A window made of thick, almost opaque, frosted glass. A long, thin, arched window...

The window.

Stan froze.

Then, somehow, his feet just started to take him across the room, towards the window... towards the machine... towards...

The computer screen. He stopped suddenly. It was an ordinary sort of screen, with bright, vivid colours, and on it was a picture. The image of a face, a face he recognized.

His own.

His eyes blurred. The image swam in and out of focus. He knew what it was – the photo snapped by the *Riverditch News* photographer when he collected his Scream City prize. But what was it doing here?

Then it was gone.

A date flashed up. Today's.

A message started to blink on and off.

WEDNESDAY OCTOBER 27

COMPLETION OF
STANLEY ARTHUR LAMPKIN

Then that, too, was gone. The screen went blank and the room went silent. Totally silent...

Until someone spoke.

"Welcome," said the voice. It was a soft, low voice, almost gentle. But it made every hair on the back of Stan's neck stand on end.

"You are a little earlier than I had anticipated," continued the voice. "But that only makes things easier for me."

It was coming from behind them. "Early – but not alone. No matter." Stan turned. So did Floella.

A figure was standing on the other side of the room. Leaning against the blank white wall, arms folded, smiling gently.

A tall figure. Thin as a rake, with the skin stretched tight and taut over his bones. His hair was white. So was his face, pale as if every drop of blood had been drained from his body.

Stan and Floella didn't move. They couldn't.

Click. The door swung shut behind them. "Locked," he said. In his hand he held something that looked like a miniature remote control device for a TV.

He looked straight at Stan through cold, pale eyes. They were eyes which didn't laugh. Eyes with no kindness behind them.

His mouth was curled up in pleasure as he studied the two of them. It was a cruel, curved mouth, with thin, mean lips. A mouth that seemed to smile as if at some secret thought.

Tap, tap, tap. The hard heels on his shiny shoes hit the floor with precise steps as he walked towards them.

Tap, tap, tap. Nearer and nearer.

He took hold of Stan's hand. His fingers were cold as ice.

"Allow me to introduce myself," he said. The words were civil, but the tone was as sinister as the hiss of a deadly snake. "My name is Fenton Maltravers."

Stan felt Floella stiffen beside him.

"Let me introduce you to my other guests," he said, his cruel mouth smiling even wider. He turned and pointed the remote controller at the bare, white wall behind him. Then he pressed one of the buttons with a bony finger.

The wall began to move. First a crack appeared in the middle, then the two halves began to separate, sliding slowly back and disappearing into the walls on either side.

Stan and Floella froze, their eyes fixed on the sight in front of them. They were staring straight into a secret room, straight into the terrified eyes of Raymond Golightly and Colin 'Crusher' Armitage.

16

TRAPPED

Raymond and Crusher were helpless, too terrified to speak. Only their eyes darted backwards and forwards from Stan to Floella, panic-stricken and begging for help.

Save us, their eyes said. *Please save us*.

Stan and Floella moved towards them. They're wearing hospital gowns, thought Stan. He clenched his fingers tight. Hospital gowns...

Both of them were sitting in what looked like dentists' chairs. Their feet and hands were held in place by metal clamps and there were straps around their chests and over their shoulders like a harness. But it was the wires that worried Stan most. The wires that were attached to their heads with what looked like thick, black sticking plasters.

Stan's eyes followed the wires to a black metal box with a row of buttons on the front. The black box hung from the ceiling on a bracket. From there, a thick cable ran to a small square screen. It was some sort of monitor. Electric green lines streaked across the screen in jagged peaks and troughs, but what they were measuring, Stan couldn't guess.

Neither Raymond nor Crusher moved a muscle. They couldn't. From the ceiling above, their terrified faces were lit by the blinding glare of fierce spotlights. Ranks of them, all giving off white, white light. And between them was an empty chair. One empty chair. Waiting.

"Yours," smiled Fenton Maltravers, following Stan's eyes. Then he smiled and pressed his remote controller.

The wall slid shut behind Stan and Floella. Click. It locked.

That's it, thought Stan. We're trapped. Trapped inside four blank walls. There's no way out. No one can help us. No one knows we're here.

"Welcome to my laboratory," said Fenton Maltravers. His voice was low and caressing, all the more terrifying for the threats that lurked just beneath the gentle tones.

A section of the wall behind Raymond and Crusher slid silently back. Stan heard Floella gasp beside him.

They were staring at a steel table. A steel table with surgical instruments laid out on it. Row upon row of sharp knives and shining scalpels, the tools of a surgeon. All laid out in neat, straight rows. Perfect. Precise. And in the wrong hands... lethal.

Fenton Maltravers walked over to the table. He picked up a long, thin scalpel. He held it to the light. The fine, sharp blade glinted brightly as he twisted and turned it in the air. He studied the effects on Stan and Floella with a sly glance from the corner of his eye. He smiled.

Then he licked his thin, mean lips, finger poised over the remote controller. He looked at Stan with a steady, concentrated gaze.

No more, thought Stan. Please. No more.

But already a panel in the wall behind him was sliding back. Already a shelf was sliding out.

Stan turned. And screamed.

A stone statue was rearing out at him. A hideous grey statue of a huge rat. A study of sheer terror. The creature's eyes were glazed with fear, its teeth were bared, its mouth was stretched back in agony. Its whole, petrified body was arched in pain, rigid with fright.

Stan began to shiver. He couldn't stop. His whole body began to shake violently. Floella clutched his arm. "Stop it," she yelled at Fenton Maltravers. "Stop it."

Fenton Maltravers threw back his head and

laughed, the same horrible laugh Stan had heard before downstairs. A laugh of cruel delight in the face of their fear.

His feet started to tap-tap across the floor towards Stan and beyond. He stretched out a bony hand to the rat. "One of my first volunteers," he whispered, his eyes staring deep into Stan's.

He stroked the terrified stone head of the rat and smiled. "Fear," he said. "Fear beyond fear." He paused and shook his head. "Too much fear can be... petrifying."

Then he laughed again, a sly laugh full of secret knowledge. His face was close to Stan's. Only a breath away. A hot, rotting breath away.

Stan shrank back. He had never felt such confusion, such helplessness, such fear. Never.

Fenton Maltravers was speaking again. It was as if he could read Stan's mind. "You are confused. Frightened," he said in a low, almost soothing voice. "All those unanswered questions... Who am I? What am I doing here? What is to become of you? You don't know what to think."

"All these things shall be answered in time," he promised. Now he was gentle, reassuring, hypnotic even, as if he was calming some small frightened creature. "But first a little film show," he whispered.

He pointed to the far wall, beyond the steel table where a giant screen was mounted on the wall. He flicked a button on the remote controller and an old TV recording started to run. A news report, read by a solemn man in a grey suit.

"A decision has today been announced in the case of Fenton Maltravers," the newsreader was saying. "This statement was issued by the medical authorities this morning."

The scene switched to a woman standing on the steps of a big building, reading from a sheet of paper. "After due consideration of all the evidence, it is the decision of this council that Fenton Maltravers is entirely unfit to practise as a surgeon, or medical practitioner of any kind."

There was a pause, as if the tape had been edited. "Neither will he be allowed to continue further in his research work, the nature of which oversteps the boundaries of good scientific practice."

Back to the newsreader. "The former eminent brain surgeon made his name in the field of research into human brain function," he said. "This led him into the controversial area of pyschosurgery, and most recently to claims that he could cure certain disorders of the mind through new, but radical, surgical procedures."

"Investigations began after misgivings were raised by his former colleague, Edwin Larousse." The picture switched to a grey haired man. A huge figure, a giant of a man. A figure Stan was sure he had seen before.

"This is a sad and regrettable moment," the man

was saying. "I have every respect for my former colleague's abilities. He has been instrumental in some truly great advancements in medical research. But this..." he shook his head. "Well, there has to come a point where medicine and science must be seen in a wider context, one of simple morality, of humanity."

A close up of Fenton Maltravers leaving the hearing flashed up on the screen. The same gaunt face, the same white hair, the same thin frame – yet he looked somehow different. More normal. More human. It was something about the eyes. The same eyes, cold and hard, but without the burning gleam of evil behind them.

"This is a grave miscarriage of justice," he began, looking straight at the camera. "My work has been misunderstood. In the future, the world *will* understand. You may rest assured that you have not seen the last of Fenton Maltravers." Then he smiled, the same sly smile.

The screen flickered and went blank.

"Indeed," whispered the sly voice softly in Stan's ear. "Now I can fulfil that promise."

17

NO ESCAPE

"I remember now," said Floella. Her eyes caught Stan's for a moment. She looked away quickly – but not quickly enough.

She's terrified, thought Stan, but there was a defiant look in her eye that he recognized too.

Fenton Maltravers studied her, with an amused smile on his face. "You remember now?"

"You were a brilliant scientist once," said Floella.

"Once?" he said, the smile freezing on his face.

"You did studies of people's brains, how they think and feel, memory, things like that," she said. Her face was ghostly white, but her cheeks were burning. Her voice sounded unnaturally loud, unnaturally high-pitched and jerky. "*Good* things."

"Good things indeed," agreed Fenton Maltravers. His lips were smiling but his eyes were like ice.

"Then something went wrong." Now her eyes were darting around the room.

She's buying time, looking for a way out, thought Stan. But it's no use. There's no escape.

His head was starting to spin now. It was hot in here, so hot, and airless. It was hard to breathe, even harder to think.

"Went wrong?" said Fenton Maltravers. He walked over to the steel table. He wiped an invisible speck of dust off it. "I was simply putting theory into practice."

"There were some brothers, they were twins..." said Floella.

"Both suffering from disorders of the mind," said Fenton Maltravers. "Psychiatric illness they call it, a wishy-washy way to describe something much more straightforward. Their brains were simply malfunctioning."

"I took it upon myself to undertake a controlled experiment. One twin was treated in the conventional way, the other agreed to surgery – to correct the malfunction, to repair the breakdown in his brain."

"But he died, didn't he," said Floella.

"He was a less robust physical specimen than he appeared to be, too weak to withstand the rigours of a pioneering surgical procedure," the scientist replied in an even voice. "But what is the death of one damaged individual compared to the importance of my work?"

Floella glared at him. "You can't talk about people like that..." she began.

"His death was regrettable of course," the scientist continued smoothly. "But it did not invalidate my research."

"But that man on the TV, he..." Floella continued.

"Edwin Larousse," interrupted Fenton Maltravers. A muscle flickered in his cheek. "Edwin Larousse," he repeated softly, picking up a sharp pair of scissors. He held them up to the light, drew them open as far as they would go, then snapped them shut. "Edwin Larousse was jealous of my success."

"He still got your work stopped," said Floella.

"He did indeed," said Fenton Maltravers. "He went missing soon after," he paused, sighing softly and shaking his head. "Such a loss."

There was silence. Stan watched the colour drain from Floella's cheeks. She's giving up, he thought. She knows we're trapped. Nothing she can say will make any difference. This man, this madman has got us here and he's not going to let us go.

"But enough of the past," said Fenton Maltravers in a quiet, calm voice. "Nothing – and no one – could be allowed to stand in my way. They should have realized that." He shook his head from side to side. "They should have realized that," he whispered sadly. But there was a small, sly glint in his eye.

Get me out of here, Stan was saying to himself. Please. Get me out of here.

"So I was forced to work here alone in secret," continued the scientist. "But with isolation came new ideas and a challenge greater than any scientist had ever dared consider."

"And how luck was with me," he whispered, an evil smile flickering across his face. "A chance discovery... how much easier it made things." Eyes glinting, he glanced at the petrified rat. "One of my first volunteers, but by no means my last." He laughed. "And now," he held out a bony hand towards Stan, "I have brought you here to..."

"No one brought us here," Floella interrupted, taking a step towards Fenton Maltravers. "We came to investigate." Her voice was loud now, but shaking, Stan could hear. Was it with anger. Or fear?

"To investigate?" said Fenton Maltravers. There was a gloating note in his voice, as if he was laughing at her. As if he had played some cruel trick she had yet to discover.

"Yes," said Floella. "We came because of the faces at the window."

Fenton Maltravers shook his head with a mocking smile. "You came because I brought you here," he said softly.

"No," said Floella, but she sounded less sure. "We saw Stan's face. That's why we came."

"Exactly," said Fenton Maltravers. "Exactly," he repeated softly. "As I knew you would. As I knew Stan would. Eventually."

There was silence for a moment. Seconds that felt like minutes before the scientist spoke again. "I know how people think. How *you* think," he whispered. "And I know why. I know exactly what it is that makes you act or feel the way you do." He paused, as if he was giving them time to absorb his words.

"Love, hate, trust, fear... these are all simple chemical reactions inside an organic machine." The scientist looked at each of his prisoners in turn. "That's all your brain is you know," he said softly. "An organic machine. There are infinite different models of course, but each one is essentially the same, rather like the engine of a motorcar."

"And once you understand how the machine – the engine – works, then you can learn how to drive. How to control. How to manipulate."

Even Floella was silent now.

"You all came here because you saw your faces at the window. *I* created those images. *I* brought you here," he said. "Different, individual responses, I grant you, but the result was the same."

"You Raymond," he gestured, lazily. "You were

sitting on the top deck of a bus travelling into town. You saw your own face staring out of a window of an unknown house."

He walked over to Raymond and smiled into the boy's terrified eyes. "It provoked a natural enquiry, natural from a mind such as yours. On your return journey you got off the bus and came here to find out more, to explain the unexplainable."

Now Fenton Maltravers bent and whispered into Raymond's ear. "You came, and much to your surprise the door was open. Your curiosity was greater than your normal sense of right and wrong and so you walked in."

Raymond's face was beaded with sweat. It had happened exactly as Fenton Maltravers had said, Stan could see.

"You want to know how I did it, don't you?" He straightened up. "Well that's my secret, but surely magnification and projection is not so very hard for you to understand, is it? With the help of a powerful computer, almost anything is possible."

Now it was Crusher's turn.

"Colin saw his face from his bedroom window," said Fenton Maltravers. "Tsk, tsk, what were you doing up so late?" he asked with a knowing smile.

Crusher didn't speak. Didn't move.

"Extra homework? Letter to a penpal?" The scientist gave a low, low laugh. "Whatever, it was as nothing compared to the sight of your own face staring out of the night sky. Have you always wanted to see your face in lights, have you Colin?"

He was taunting now, but the bulky figure trapped in the chair didn't move.

"So, was it vanity that brought you here? The pleasure at seeing your own features displayed for all to see... or *insecurity?*" He spat out the word, "Was it the fear that this was some some sort of practical joke? You don't like jokes do you Colin? You don't like having tricks played on you, do you? But whatever the reason, you came all the same."

Tears rolled out of Crusher's eyes and down his cheeks. His whole body shook with silent sobs as he stared down at the clamps around his wrists.

"Now Stanley," the scientist continued. Stan held his breath. "Well, we know all about Stanley." He turned to Stan.

"You saw them both, didn't you?" said the scientist. "But you didn't trust yourself, didn't trust what you saw. You might have come earlier. You might have done something. Who knows, you might have scuppered my plans." He gave a false laugh. "So what stopped you?" He paused, but he wasn't expecting Stan to answer.

"Fear," whispered Fenton Maltravers in Stan's ear. "That most powerful of human responses. It was your fear that stopped you. As I knew it would."

Stan looked at Raymond and Crusher. I failed them, he thought. I was their only chance of escape and I failed them. And now it's too late.

"So what brought you, Stanley?" the scientist continued, turning to Floella with a smile. "It was, of course, your sister's *lack* of fear, her boldness, that brought you here. In the end."

Stan flashed a glance at Floella, standing rigid, not moving an inch. A picture of home flashed into his head. Him, Dad, Floella, all round the fire, laughing. Tears sprang to his eyes. He felt small, terrified. *I want to go home,* said a voice in his head. *Dad, where are you? I want to go home.*

Floella stepped in front of him. A small patch of red had returned to her cheeks.

"So this window," she began, "has some kind of irresistible hypnotic power or something, which draws people here, is that what you're saying?" Her voice wobbled. She was struggling.

"No, my dear," smiled the scientist. "That is what *you* are saying."

And then he laughed again, that low, horrible laugh. "But in the end, how you got here doesn't matter one way or the other."

He's right, thought Stan. It doesn't. We're here. We're trapped. And something awful is about to happen...

"Stanley," said Fenton Maltravers. "It is time to begin."

18

BRAIN POWER

Fenton Maltravers held out a gown to Stan. Stan took it. He had no choice.

"What you are now involved in goes beyond anything ever believed possible," said the scientist. His eyes were trained on Stan. They were deadly serious. "You are now about to play a small part in the most important development in human history."

He looked slowly from Raymond... to Crusher... to Stan. His eyes almost glittered.

"The creation of a perfect machine," he said softly. "The fusion of three very different types of brain, drawing on the particular strength of each and discarding the weakness of all."

No one spoke a word. Raymond and Crusher looked blank, as if someone had turned off a switch inside their heads. Stan fixed his eyes on Fenton Maltravers, on his white, bloodless face and his cold, soulless eyes.

He's mad, whispered the small voice inside Stan's head. *Insane. You're in the hands of a lunatic. You have to do something!* But Stan couldn't move.

The silence was broken by Floella. "You're completely crazy," she cried. "Crazy."

The scientist shook his head. "Misunderstood," he said, turning to her. "Misunderstood." He laughed a low mocking laugh.

Wake me up, Stan was begging to himself. Tell me I'm dreaming. Tell me it's not real. I can't take any more.

"You are the raw material," the scientist continued. "But nature can only do so much. The rest is up to me. I shall transform that raw material. After all these years, I am ready at last." He smiled. But no one else did.

"In less than what is left of your short lives, I shall achieve what the evolutionary process might only accomplish over hundreds of thousands of years..."

He stopped and the corners of his thin, mean mouth curled upwards. "No. I shall achieve what the evolutionary process could *never* accomplish... the creation of a perfect brain."

The room went silent, but Stan hardly noticed. The scientist's words were spinning round and round in his head.

"The perfect machine..." continued Fenton Maltravers. "Able to harness emotions. Able to turn them on and off like a light, with a switch, operated by logic."

He walked over to the empty chair and beckoned to Stan. "And the key to this power? Control of that most basic, and strongest, of all reactions – fear."

"FEAR," he repeated. "Something Stanley knows all too well."

"Stan's not afraid," Floella butted in. "None of us are. You're insane."

But I *am* afraid, thought Stan. I'm more afraid than I've ever been before.

"Fear," said Fenton Maltravers softly. "So powerful, yet so wild and unpredictable."

Floella's hands were bunched up by her sides. Stan could see her clenching and unclenching her fists. But she didn't speak.

"Just consider for a moment, the power of fear," continued Fenton Maltravers. "It is at the root of all human instinct. Take primitive man. Fear of his enemy taught him to run, fear of starvation taught him to kill, fear of death taught him to survive."

Why doesn't he stop? thought Stan. Stop all this talking and get on with it. Anything is better than this. The waiting.

"But it can destroy too," continued the scientist. "Fear of tomorrow, fear of the unknown, fear of a wealth of trivial things... these things can cripple, cause a total breakdown in the function of the mind."

He paused. His cold eyes stared slowly at each of them in turn.

"But imagine the power of a brain able to harness its fear. To control it. To use the impulses generated for strength instead of for weakness. Imagine the perfect brain... my perfect brain."

Floella couldn't bear any more, "Why these three?" she shouted. "Why choose these three?"

Fenton Maltravers smiled. He looked at Raymond, then Crusher, then Stan. "For many things," he said softly. "For the qualities each in turn can bring to my work. For the combination of science, strength and imagination they represent. And most of all, for their reactions to fear."

"Raymond brings logic to bear. He tries to analyse, tries to understand. Colin refuses to admit its existence, yet like so many of his type, he is perhaps the most fearful of all," Fenton Maltravers paused briefly.

"But it is Stanley here who interests me most." He began to walk towards Stan, taking neat, precise steps.

"He is the most complex and the most contradictory. He denies his fears but in doing so, he reinforces them. He generates new fears in an effort to dispel old ones. He shrinks from fear, yet confronts it. Yes, I suspect of you all, it is Stanley who is the bravest. For without fear, there is no courage."

He stroked his hand gently across Stan's forehead. "A marvellous specimen," he whispered. "A glorious range of chemical responses, a perfect base for remodelling. For modifications," he smiled, staring first at Raymond, then Crusher, "and additions."

He leaned forward. "You, Stanley," he whispered. "You shall be my first, my working prototype."

Stan stared blankly ahead. He could hear the voice speaking, but he wasn't listening to the words. He didn't want to know what they meant.

"And still a child," the scientist continued.

"Stan's not a *child*, he's nearly..." Floella protested.

"Children," Fenton Maltravers continued, "have greater potential. The brain is sufficiently developed but its capacity is still enormous, uncluttered with the empty thoughts and petty concerns of adulthood."

"No girls, I see," muttered Floella.

"The weaker sex. Greatly overestimated these days, but in my experience inferior," Fenton Maltravers replied, turning away from her.

He picked up a syringe from the steel table and beckoned to Stan.

All this will be over soon, promised a new voice in Stan's head. He took a step forward.

"Don't do. Don't do it..." Floella was whispering.

Stan looked at Floella. Her voice had sounded choked, desperate. There were tears in her terrified eyes. He wanted to tell her not to cry, not to get so upset. There was nothing she could do. Nothing any of them could do. *It will be over soon,* promised the new voice inside his head,

He wanted to tell her it was better just to give in. Give up. Why fight it? He wanted to tell her... but he couldn't. All he could do was take a step towards the empty chair. Fenton Maltravers watched, with a gleam of satisfaction in his eyes.

"NO," yelled Floella. "What you're doing is WRONG. It's EVIL."

Fenton Maltravers raised his hand, then stopped mid motion. "Wrong? Right? Who are you to say?"

"Cutting out bits of people's brains IS wrong. Anyone will tell you that..." Floella exploded.

There was an amused smile on the scientist's face. "Cutting out people's brains? My techniques require a little more sophistication than that," he said. "One small incision, one point of entry. Here," he touched her forehead with one cold bony finger. "Or here," his finger moved to her eye. "Direct access to the frontal lobes of the brain."

Floella flinched and edged backwards, closer to the wall.

"But first, a little stimulation." He pointed to the monitor screen with the jagged green lines. "Brain activity of the highest intensity is crucial to the success of my operation."

With one swift movement he turned on his heels and pointed his remote controller at the black box that hung from the ceiling.

"A remarkable piece of micro-electronic engineering," he smiled. "It measures the level of electro-chemical activity while stimulating the brain at the same time, implanting messages – ideas – deep inside the brain. Images, suggestions, delusions, all tailor made to trigger a response. And you know what response I mean, don't you..."

He laughed.

"I call it my Medusa," the scientist said softly. "My Medusa." He was whispering, talking to himself. Was this some private joke? Floella couldn't tell. She didn't understand, but she hadn't given up. Not yet.

"Don't you feel *anything*?" she asked. "Guilt? Compassion?" There was a sob in her voice, but Stan didn't notice. He couldn't hear her any more.

"Why should I?" said Fenton Maltravers, turning to Stan. He beckoned. No smile. Nothing.

Stan's feet were moving slowly towards the empty chair. He felt tired, so tired. The chair was straight in front of him. He was ready.

"You can't see, can you?" said Fenton Maltravers to Floella. "You're simply not capable. Typical of the limitations of the female mind." He turned away.

But Floella did see. All too clearly.

She saw a once brilliant mind perverted by its utter and total belief in itself. A mind completely lacking in humanity.

"You'll get caught," she said, desperate now.

Fenton Maltravers shook his head slowly. "I don't think so," he said.

Stan was five steps away from the chair.

"Someone will find us," Floella shouted.

"I doubt it," Fenton Maltravers replied, with a smile. "Any more than they found the others."

He laughed. A cruel, evil laugh. "I told you this was a remarkable machine," he whispered. "A machine with unimaginable capacity... if I leave it running."

His eyes swivelled across the room and rested for a moment on the statue of the rat. The crazed, terrified figure of a poor helpless animal, frozen in fear. Petrified. Cast in cold, grey stone forever. Then he turned back to Stan.

Only three steps away from the chair now.

Two.

One.

Fenton Maltravers gave a triumphant smile.

"Nothing can stop me now."

Stan sat down and held out his arms for the buckles. His eyes were open, but he couldn't see Floella standing against the wall, watching, fists clenched, breathing fast and thinking hard. *This is it,* said the new voice in his head. *It's almost over. Whatever is about to happen, it's almost over.*

But Floella was alert and thinking fast. He wouldn't defeat them. She wouldn't let him. She had to find a way.

Fenton Maltravers took a step back. He seemed to have forgotten that Floella was still in the room. She was irrelevant to his scheme. He stood still, silently studying the three figures now slumped in front of him, mesmerized by fear.

Then Fenton Maltravers lifted his arm. In his hand he held the remote controller. His finger was poised. Did he press it? Stan looked straight into his eyes... "Help me," he screamed.

19

COUNTDOWN

"Noooooooooooooooo!" A voice screamed out. It was a wild, animal scream of rage and anger. Floella hardly recognized it as her own. There was a horrible cracking sound.

Fenton Maltravers slumped to the floor at the foot of Stan's chair. Stan blinked, dimly aware of Floella standing in front of him, motionless, her mouth open wide. In her hands she was clutching the heavy stone statue of the rat. She was staring down at the floor, stunned by what she had done.

There was blood on the grey stone head of the rat, trickling down over its bared stone teeth. Trickling over Floella's white knuckles and onto the floor.

There wasn't a sound in the room.

Stan stared down at the body on the floor. It didn't move.

He looked over at Raymond and Crusher. Their faces were white. White as the wall behind them.

Stan's breath came out in a great sob. He pulled his arms free of the unfastened clamps and buried his head in his hands. Was it over? Was it really all over?

He stumbled out of the chair and went over to Crusher. He fumbled with the clamps that held him and pulled the wires from his head. Crusher opened his mouth, tried to speak, but only a croak came out of his mouth.

Raymond was the same. He just sat there, shaking and shaking and shaking. Beyond words, beyond thought, beyond anything.

And still Floella stood motionless, eyes fixed on the floor, clutching the statue. Stan gently removed it from her hands and put it on the shelf. The sticky red liquid was smeared all over his hands.

"Floella," he said, shaking her gently. But she didn't look at him, just stared down at the drops on her hands.

Then Fenton Maltravers opened one eye...

And the other.

He looked up at Stan. His eyes were blank at first, but he was regaining consciousness. The cold glint was beginning to return. The thin lips were starting to move. The evil was flooding back.

Fenton Maltravers started to stagger to his feet. He was standing now. Stan looked around for help. The others were motionless, in shock. *Do something,* said a voice in Stan's head – the old, familiar voice. *Do something. You're the only one who can.*

Stan put his head down and ran, like a charging bull. He ran at the staggering figure of Fenton Maltravers with a strength he didn't know he possessed. He ran with one thought in his head. This is our only chance. Our only chance to get out of here. Life... or death. Him... or us.

Stan's head made contact. The scientist was knocked off his feet and flung backwards into the empty chair. Quick! The straps, the buckles, the clamps... Stan snapped every one into place.

Then he stood back and looked at Fenton Maltravers. "Let me go," said the man, staring into his eyes.

But it didn't work. The cold, cruel eyes seemed to have no power over Stan now.

"Set me free and I shall let you all go," he said, but his voice was no longer so smooth, so sure.

"Set me free," he said again, louder this time, desperate, pleading.

Stan turned away. "Let's go," he said to the others. "Now!"

"You can't leave me here," cried Fenton Maltravers. "Not with the machine switched on."

Stan looked at Floella. She was picking up the wires, the wires that ran to the black box. Her hands were moving swiftly, angrily, as she attached the electrodes to the scientist's head, his white hair covered in fresh blood from the wound.

Stan gaped in horror. "What are you doing?"

"Nothing more than he was going to do to you," she said, with a furious look on her face.

"Come on," yelled Stan, grabbing at Raymond's sleeve.

"Don't do this," cried the scientist. "You don't realize what the machine will do... the images magnify... fears expand... the power intensifies." His eyes were panic-stricken, his white face taut with fear. "You must set me free."

Stan grabbed the remote controller from where it had fallen on the floor. He pointed it at the walls and pressed the buttons at random. There was no response. He jabbed at them again. At last. The walls were sliding back. Click. The door was unlocked.

"RUN!" yelled Stan, shaking Crusher who seemed glued to the spot. "Just get out of here. NOW."

"Stop the machine!" screamed Fenton Maltravers. "Don't you realize the power of fear... Stop the machine," he screamed again, his mouth contorted in a terrible cry of despair.

They ran.

Out of the door, down the spiral steps, along the dark corridor, down the staircase, through the hallway, past the table and chairs, past the inscription above the old stone fireplace, and out into the night.

They took lungfuls of cold, fresh air. Then, without another word, they stumbled out through the garden, gaining speed with every step, past the stone statues and into the woods.

And then the screams began. Scream after terrible scream rang out, carried on the breeze, following them as they ran. Wild, savage howls, like the terrified cries of an animal at bay, ripping through the silence of the night. Who would have guessed they were the agonized screams of a man?

Suddenly there was silence. The screaming had stopped. Now there was just the wind in the trees and the thud, thud of their feet on the ground, as they stumbled towards the safety of the glowing lights coming from the houses in The Glades.

Home, thought Stan. In a minute we'll be home.

20

LATER

When the police went to investigate, they found the house and the room at the top of the spiral staircase just as Stan and the others had described it. The open door, the chairs, the machinery, the surgical instruments, the blood stains. Everything.

But there was no sign of Fenton Maltravers. Not a trace. The police questioned them all again very carefully.

Crusher and Raymond found it difficult to remember much of their ordeal and Stan's memory of events was hazy in the middle. But Floella remembered everything, every detail.

She told them about the things Fenton

Maltravers had said, his scheme and his threats. And she told them how she had hit him over the head with the statue, in self defence. How it was the only thing she could have done.

Stan told them how Fenton Maltravers had regained consciousness and how they had strapped him to the chair, so they could escape.

And the police said they believed them.

Fenton Maltravers was never found. But on one of the chairs, the straps were broken, ripped from their bolts as if wrenched by some incredible strength. The clamps were bent and twisted and all the wires were pulled and torn. The police found them hanging loose from the black metal box. And on the screen, there was nothing but a straight, still, electric green line. That was all. There was no sign of Fenton Maltravers.

Anywhere.

Later, many months later, towards the end of the summer holidays, Stan and Floella decided to go back to the old house.

From Stan's bedroom window, they could just see the old house through the trees. The windows were shuttered. It still looked deserted, but in the bright summer sunshine, it all seemed somehow less frightening. The horrors of the house and that terrible night were far behind them. Something that had happened a long time ago.

They followed the winding path through the woods, climbed the rusty iron gate and found the track through the trees. They passed the stone slab, with its strange message still untouched by moss and free from the tangle of creepers that smothered everything else. They reached the edge of the abandoned garden where the first statue stood pointing...

And that was where they stopped.

There was another statue in the thick, long grass, blocking their path. It hadn't been there before. Stan was certain. This was a new statue...

It was the figure of a man, a man whose features were grotesquely distorted by fear.

A tall, thin man with his arms flung outwards in horror, and his legs outstretched, as if he was running. Escaping from something.

A man with a cruel curved mouth stretched back in a ghastly grin of despair.

A man with one long bony finger stretched forward.

Pointing...

Pointing straight at Stan, while the sunlight glinted in his cold, stone eyes.

USBORNE SPINECHILLERS

Letters from the Grave

When a new girl at school is the victim of bullying, dark forces from the spirit world are unleashed. An invisible hand writing mysterious messages on the blackboard is just one of a horrifying chain of events that quickly spirals out of control.

USBORNE SPINECHILLERS

CLOCK OF DOOM

When an ancient curse is accidentally triggered, Time itself becomes the enemy. There's only one boy who can stand against the forces of evil. But will he *really* be able to stop the dreaded Clock of Doom?